LAMPSTANDS OF GOD SERIES

ENOCH
LAMPSTAND *of* GOD

ERIK FREE

ENOCH
Lampstand of God

In a world of chaos and darkness, one man will be a beacon of hope.

Enoch awakens in a desolate land, echoes of divine wisdom flooding his mind from three millennia spent in the presence of God. As he grapples with confusion and the heavy burden of his purpose, Enoch embarks on a perilous journey to reclaim faith and fight against the oppressive Green World Church.

Guided by angels and armed with the truth, Enoch encounters both allies and enemies, from a healed beggar in a bustling city to spies lurking within his own ranks. As demonic forces conspire with their earthly counterparts, the lines between good and evil blur, thrusting Enoch into a cosmic battle that will test his resolve and faith.

With the fiery presence of the divine and the rising threat of the Anti-Christ looming on the horizon, Enoch must unite the Commandment Keepers and confront the darkness gathering around them. In this gripping tale of struggle, redemption, and unwavering faith, can one man's light shine through the gathering storm?

Join Enoch in "Lampstand of God" and witness the unfolding of an epic saga where faith becomes the ultimate weapon against the shadows of despair.

DEDICATION

Dedicated to the memory of Fish$teak. Love and miss you brother.
"When life throws you curves, just lean into them" Fish$teak 3AM

Copyright © 2024 by Erik Free
All rights reserved.
No portion of this book may be reproduced in any form without written permission
from the publisher or author, except as permitted by U.S. copyright law

FOWARD

Foreword by Dr. Imus B. Berryhill,

In a world often overshadowed by doubt and discord, the timeless truths of faith can serve as a guiding light. It is with great enthusiasm that I introduce "Enoch, Lampstands of God," a profound exploration into the depths of spirituality and the intricate tapestry of divine purpose woven through our lives.

This remarkable series invites readers to embark on a transformative journey, illuminating the pathways of belief and understanding. The author skillfully navigates the complexities of human experience, employing rich narrative and vivid character development to breathe life into theological concepts that resonate deeply within the heart and mind.

Each page serves as a lampstand, shining brightly the illuminating truths that have guided countless individuals throughout history. These stories remind us that we are not alone in our searches for meaning; rather, we are part of a grand narrative that unites us all in our shared struggles and triumphs.

As we delve into this engaging work, I encourage each reader to approach it with an open heart and an inquisitive mind. Explore the mysteries of faith, grapple with the challenges of existence, and, ultimately, find solace and strength in the divine presence that surrounds you.

May "Enoch, Lampstands of God" not only inspire your intellect but also ignite a flame within your spirit, guiding you toward a deeper understanding of the interplay between humanity and the divine.

Yours in faith and scholarship,

Dr. Imus B. Berryhill Th.D

AUTHOR'S NOTE

Thank you

As you delve into "Lampstands of God series," it's essential to understand that this narrative is a work of fiction inspired by biblical passages and themes. The journey of Enoch and Elijah and the various characters within this story draw from the rich tapestry of scripture while exploring the timeless struggles between light and darkness, faith and despair.

While the events and characters in this book are fictional and designed for storytelling, they reflect the underlying truths found in the Bible. I will further explore the true nature of God's Lampstands in an upcoming nonfiction book, delving into the enigmatic 1260-day prophecy and unpacking the profound biblical meanings behind the Lampstands.

In the forthcoming works, readers can expect a deeper exploration of these spiritual concepts, intended to provide clarity and understanding that enriches the narrative you've just experienced in this fictional journey. I hope that all these works will inspire reflection and deepen your connection to these timeless truths and hope that the Love of God will embrace you always and forever.

Thank you for joining me on this adventure!

www.erikfree.com

CONTENTS

Prologue	1
Chapter 1	3
Chapter 2	10
Chapter 3	18
Chapter 4	27
Chapter 5	36
Chapter 6	45
Chapter 7	54
Chapter 8	65
Chapter 9	78
Chapter 10	94
Chapter 11	103
Chapter 12	111
Chapter 13	119
Chapter 14	128
Chapter 15	134

Chapter 16	142
Chapter 17	151
Chapter 18	160
Chapter 19	169
Chapter 20	183
Chapter 21	192
Chapter 22	198
Chapter 23	204
Chapter 24	207

PROLOGUE

The gentle flow of the river of life shimmered under the celestial glow of the heavens, casting a multitude of colors that danced across the ethereal landscape. Enoch walked along its banks, the cool waters lapping softly at the edges of the path, and the air filled with a harmonious melody that only the divine realm could compose. It was a sanctuary of peace, a stark contrast to what awaited him.

As he continued, a mighty figure approached him: Michael, the Archangel. Radiant wings unfurled behind him like a sunrise breaking through dawn's haze, and his presence exuded strength and reassurance. "Enoch," Michael greeted, his voice a blend of authority and compassion. "We must speak about your mission."

Enoch paused, his heart heavy with apprehension. "Michael, do I truly have to return?" he asked, gazing into the river's depths. The waters mirrored his unease, rippling as if responding to his reluctance. "It has been three millennia. The world is not as it was."

Michael stepped closer, his eyes piercing yet kind. "I understand your hesitation, but the need is great. The world you once knew has changed, yes, but the light within you remains untouched. You will guide those who wander in shadows."

"Others revered me here, and I felt connected to the divine," Enoch murmured. "How can I fulfill this task in a desolate, wicked place?"

"The wisdom you gained here is your strength," Michael assured him. "You carry the essence of Heaven within you. Your experiences, your compassion, they are your lampstand, illuminating the path for others. They will look to you and find solace in your presence."

Enoch's thoughts swirled. The comfort of Heaven felt like a warm embrace. He was reluctant to leave. "What if I fail?" he questioned, vulnerability seeping into his tone.

Michael placed a reassuring hand on his shoulder. "Failure is a part of every journey. It is not the destination but the courage to step forward that matters. You are not alone. I, and many others, will be by your side, guiding you."

Taking a deep breath, Enoch finally nodded, surrendering to the inevitability of his mission. The river flowed on, a reminder of the cycle of life, while the stars above twinkled with expectation.

"Very well," Enoch said, determination beginning to kindle within him. "I will go. But I do so knowing the weight of the task ahead."

"Then let us prepare," Michael replied, his wings lifting slightly as he fell into stride beside Enoch. "The world awaits its Lampstand."

As they journeyed, the sight of Heaven dissolved, giving way to the earth's call, a prelude to trials that would test Enoch's limits.

CHAPTER 1

Enoch sat up, aware of the stench of old filth in the small mud-brick room, only twelve feet to a side. "What new world have they sent me to this time?" he thought. He got off the bed, if one could call it that, a few planks of wood tied together with rope and wire and covered with a thin mattress of straw. "Where am I?" he thought, trying to clear his head. His feet found the ground. "Great, at least this one has a solid ground," he said. A rag or sack covered the window, and the door only reached six feet high. "Note to self, duck."

Surveying the space, he noticed a small wooden table accompanied by a single chair, its old yellow plastic covering tattered at the front right corner, with stuffing spilling out. The two supports that once held the backrest were missing.

On the table rested two mason jars, both filled with clear liquid. He rose, swaying slightly. "Shake it off, man," he told himself. He noticed a piece of paper on the table. The three steps he took toward the table reminded him of the years that had weighed on his knees and back. The sound of snapping, crackling, and popping echoed through the desolate little dwelling. He reached for the note, brushing away a month's worth of dust with a shake and a quick blow. He deciphered the scrawled coal writing: "Take what you need, give what you can, good water in the well."

Setting the note back down, he reached for one of the mason jars containing the clear liquid, unscrewing the lid with a popping sound that resonated throughout the small room. "Good water in the well," the note had said. He took a sniff; it was odorless. Dipping his finger into the liquid and bringing it to his lips, he thought, "No stinging or numbness—that's a good sign." Tentatively, he took a small sip, feeling the cool, refreshing water wash over his tongue. He drained half of the mason jar, rinsing the dryness from his newly awakened mouth. Turning, he approached the window, pulling aside the sack to glimpse the outside world.

Before him lay the abandoned, sun-scorched mountains of the desert, jagged and steep, their rocky faces framing the horizon. A clear blue sky stretched above them, and the warm earth tones scattered across the land, with shrubs and cacti dotting the sandy ground—an area that hadn't welcomed human footsteps in quite some time. Stepping back, he finished the water from the mason jar and returned it to the table.

He surveyed the room again and saw a black backpack by the bed. Curious, he placed it on the bed and unzipped it. Inside, he found tan cargo pants, a desert-colored long-sleeve shirt, hiking boots in his size, and a desert cloak. He also found two empty water bottles, which he thought could be useful. In the front compartment, he discovered a small compass, a folded map in a plastic bag, and some paracord. Flipping the backpack, he found a large Damascus Steel Bowie knife in a pocket. He found nothing in the other pockets or compartments. He put on the cargo pants over his shorts and commented that they were a bit big. Then he put on the shirt, which was two sizes too big. After securing the buttons, he sat on the bed to put on the boots.

While doing so, he noticed a polished wooden staff on the floor. It was a seventy-inch long rod made from olive wood, beautifully crafted. He picked it up and tapped it on the ground, finding it sturdy.

Placing the rod next to the backpack, and took another look at his inventory: backpack, knife, rod, two water bottles, map, compass, midsize plastic Zip-Lock Bag, and Paracord.

"Take what you need, leave what you can," he recalled from the note. Placing the cloak around his shoulders and sliding his arms through the provided openings and remembering to duck, he stepped through the doorway.

Outside, he estimated it to be around noon, the sun high in the sky, and the arid desert temperature hovering between sixty and seventy degrees. To his right, he spotted the well, constructed from local stones stacked atop one another, standing about three feet high on a flat rock foundation, both sand-etched from years of shifting grains.

His thoughts drifted back to when Jesus spoke with the Samaritan woman at Jacob's well thousands of years ago—how weary He was from His journey from Judea to Galilee, resting at that well in Sychar, waiting for a woman to draw water. He had asked her, "Will you give me a drink?" The Samaritan woman had replied, "You are a Jew, and I am a Samaritan woman. How can you ask me for a drink?" Such racial divides persisted during that era, born of shared blood yet separated by belief. His response was so profound: "If you knew the gift of God and who it is that asks you for a drink, you would have asked him, and he would have given you Living Water." "Living Water, man," he said aloud. "If only everyone else could understand," he thought.

Approaching the well, he noticed a bucket attached to a rope, but remembered he had left his two water bottles inside. "Great," he muttered under his breath. He turned to head back in, colliding with the doorway and nearly knocking himself out. Shaking off the cobwebs from his tear-dampened eyes, he retrieved his two water bottles and the mason jar he had used, heading back out to the well to fill them all. (Take what you need, leave what you can) echoed in his mind as he returned the jar to the table, picked up the piece of coal he had noticed earlier from the windowsill, and wrote on the note, "Took what I needed, left a blessing for those to follow." He knelt and prayed to Jehovah, our God, the Creator of Heaven and Earth, asking for a blessing on this humble hut—that good water may continue to flow and that it may stand as shelter for the weary in need. He thanked Him for providing all that was needed for this new awakening.

Rising, he placed the two water bottles back into the backpack, attached the ram-handled knife to the left side of the pack using the straps, and tucked the compass into the front pouch. Taking the map out, he laid it on the table, orienting it north by noting that the sun had dipped, casting shadows on his back and slightly to his left. "Yeah right, like I know where I'm at?" he said aloud. Joshua Tree National Park was the first thing that caught his eye. "Joshua, how well I remember his adventure—how he led Israel across the Jordan with the Ark of the Covenant, the walls of Jericho, with the sound of trumpets." A smile spread across his face. "Wow, how we follow such an amazing God; if only everyone else could understand," he thought. Folding the map, he returned it to the ziplock bag and slid it into the front pouch of the backpack. "Daylight is burning; time to go." He grabbed the map, rolled it up, and tucked it into the right pocket of the backpack.

Throwing the backpack over his shoulders, he made his way to the door, remembering to duck this time as he stepped outside. "Jehovah, guide my way," he called into the vast openness surrounding him. After walking about twenty feet past the well, he noticed a pillar of cloud forming to the north. A smile of joy lit up his face as he recognized that Jehovah and Yahshua were with him. "I know this story—follow the cloud," he said with gratitude. "Here I am, a lampstand with no plan," he mused as he took his first steps in pursuit of the pillar of cloud that Jehovah and Yahshua had provided.

* * *

Enoch's gaze lingered on the pillar of cloud, his heart beating in rhythm with a newfound purpose. With the weight of his backpack settling against his shoulders, he trod across the sunbaked earth; the sand shifting beneath his worn boots. Each step left a distinct imprint, a testament to his passage through this desolate land.

As he moved, the silence of the desert enveloped him, broken only by the occasional whisper of wind stirring the dust. He passed remnants of civilization—cracked foundations and fallen broken walls that whispered stories of a forgotten past. The stark beauty of the ruins tugged at his memory, echoes of lives once vibrant now lost to time.

He reached a point where the ground rose, and there, half-buried in the sand, lay an ancient coin. Centuries of wind and weather wore its edges smooth. Enoch picked it up, rubbing away the grit to reveal faded inscriptions—a language he recognized but from an era long since vanished.

He tucked the coin into his pocket, feeling its weight against his leg as he resumed his journey. The terrain grew more rugged, with rocks jutting out like bones from the earth's flesh. Each step became more deliberate as Enoch navigated through this graveyard of nature's making.

Ahead, where land met sky, the pillar seemed to beckon him onward, a silent guide amidst an unspoken history. Enoch pressed forward, curiosity and resolve intermingling within him. Though the path was unclear and his destination unknown, he trusted in the guidance that unfolded before him.

A hawk circled overhead, its sharp cry piercing the quietude as if announcing Enoch's progress to the heavens. He watched its graceful flight until it disappeared beyond a ridge crowned with jagged silhouettes.

As evening approached, shadows stretched across the landscape like dark fingers reaching for something just out of grasp. The temperature dropped with the sun's descent, painting the sky in hues of orange and pink.

Enoch's breath formed small clouds in front of him as he exhaled into the cooling air of the evening. Ahead, the pillar appeared to solidify with the waning light, becoming more distinct against the darkening backdrop.

He reached a clearing where cacti stood guard like sentinels over a sea of pebbles and sand. Here he paused, considering his next move while taking in the surrounding stillness. The pillar seemed closer now—its presence a constant amidst shifting sands and changing skies—a steadfast companion on this journey toward an unknown horizon.

Enoch surveyed the clearing, noting how the cacti created natural barriers against the wind. He shrugged off his pack and rolled his shoulders, easing the tension from hours of walking. He noticed the ground beneath his feet was packed hard, perfect for a night's rest.

From his pack, he pulled a threadbare blanket and spread it across the earth. The fabric's once-vibrant patterns had faded to muted browns and grays, matching the surrounding landscape. He arranged stones in a circle, preparing a spot for a fire, though wood would be scarce in this barren place.

The sun dipped lower, casting long shadows across his makeshift camp. He gathered what dried vegetation he could find—brittle stems and sun-bleached brush. The plants crackled as he broke them into manageable pieces.

A spark from his flint caught the tinder. The flames cast a warm glow across the clearing, pushing back the encroaching darkness. Heat radiated from the small fire, a welcome respite from the desert's cooling air.

Enoch settled onto his blanket, legs crossed, his back against his pack. The pillar of cloud remained visible in the dying light, a constant presence on the horizon. Stars emerged overhead, pinpricks of light in an endless expanse of darkening sky.

He pulled the coin from his pocket, turning it over in his hands. The firelight caught its edges, highlighting the worn symbols that spoke of ages past. The metal felt warm against his palm, a small piece of history anchoring him to this desolate present.

The fire popped, sending sparks dancing into the night air. Around him, the desert settled into its nocturnal rhythm. A gentle breeze stirred the sand, whispering across the clearing. Enoch gave thanks for the day and went to sleep..

CHAPTER 2

The first rays of dawn painted the horizon when a thin layer of white coated the ground around Enoch's makeshift camp. He knelt down, running his fingers through the frost-like substance. The familiar sight brought a smile to his face—manna, bread from heaven.

Gathering the delicate flakes into his zip-lock bag, memories of ancient Israel's wanderings flooded his mind. Their struggles, their complaints, their lessons in faith. But unlike them, he had no implements to bake with, no way to prepare it as they had.

A flash of light interrupted his thoughts. A figure materialized before him, radiating celestial energy. Enoch's face lit up with recognition.

"Zophiel, my old friend." Enoch stepped forward, embracing the angel.

Zophiel's wings shimmered in the morning light. "How exciting that the time has finally arrived." His voice carried the weight of ages, yet sparkled with anticipation.

"Indeed." Enoch adjusted his pack. "How is the Anointed One doing?" Enoch replied.

Zophiel reached into his robes and produced a package wrapped in leaves that gleamed with an otherworldly sheen. "He sends His greetings, along with this gift." He handed the parcel to Enoch.

Enoch lays his staff next to him and unwrapped the leaves, revealing meat that seemed to glow with its own light. "Is this from the trees on the river of healing in Elysium?"

"The very same." Zophiel's eyes twinkled. "It will sustain you on your journey."

"Come sit with me a moment, Lampstand. Let me tell you the message from our King Yahshua," Zophiel said, setting down two large rocks near a shade tree.

Zophiel and Enoch settled on the rocks, the morning sun casting long shadows across the barren landscape.

"The world has changed, Lampstand. Humanity walks in darkness, their hearts turned to stone." Zophiel's wings drooped. "They've built towers of glass and steel, reaching for the heavens, yet they've forgotten who placed the stars above them."

Enoch's shoulders slumped as he surveyed the desolate horizon. "The temples - where are they?"

"Abandoned. Replaced with shrines to commerce and entertainment. They worship screens that fit in their palms, algorithms that predict their desires, and artificial beings they've created in their own image." Zophiel traced patterns in the dust. "The Creator's name is but a whisper in forgotten texts."

"Even after the flood? After all He did for them?" Enoch's voice cracked.

"They explain away the rainbow as mere refraction of light. The great deluge? A local flooding event, they say. Your own walk with God? A metaphor." Zophiel's face hardened. "They've replaced divine wisdom with their own understanding."

Enoch unwrapped the glowing meat, breaking off a small piece. "And what of the springs of living water? The seas He separated from the land?"

"Polluted with plastics and chemicals. They harvest the seas empty, while claiming dominion without stewardship. The springs run dry as they drain ancient aquifers." Zophiel gestured to the barren landscape. "They've forgotten He holds all things together by the word of His power."

"The Everlasting One..." Enoch's voice trailed off as he remembered walking with God in the cool of day, seeing creation through His eyes. "They've traded immortality for temporary pleasures."

"Yes. They measure time in quarterly profits and viral trends, blind to the eternal." Zophiel placed a hand on Enoch's shoulder. "That's why you're here, Lampstand. The world needs to remember."

Zophiel's wings shifted, casting prismatic patterns across the ground. "The followers of Babylon have spread their tendrils far and wide. They've twisted the sacred calendar, moved the Sabbath to Sun's day."

Enoch's brow furrowed. "They worship the created rather than the Creator?"

"Their temples point west, to catch the setting sun. They've erected obelisks in every major city, symbols of the ancient sky god. The winter solstice has become their highest celebration." Zophiel traced a circle in the dust. "They call it Christmas now, claiming it honors the birth of the Messiah."

"But Yahshua wasn't born in winter." Enoch's voice carried a note of pain.

"No. They've changed the times, the seasons, the laws. Easter replaced Passover, named after Ishtar, the queen of fertility. Sunday replaced the seventh-day Sabbath." Zophiel's face darkened. "They've grafted pagan rituals onto holy convocations, creating a new religion that appears godly but denies His power."

Enoch picked up a handful of dust, letting it slip through his fingers. "The same spirit of Babel - reaching for heaven on their own terms."

"Their leaders wear the purple and scarlet of ancient Babylon. They carry the symbols - the fish of Dagon, the cross of Tammuz." Zophiel's wings folded closer. "They've built a system that appears righteous but serves the prince of the power of the air."

"How many still remember the true name?" Enoch asked.

"Few. They've replaced it with titles and substitutes. The calendar they follow bears the names of Roman gods - Januar, Mars, Juno. Even the days of the week honor Norse and Saxon deities."

Zophiel's wings darkened, casting shadows across the ground. "The cup of iniquity is full. Those who drink from Babylon's golden chalice will taste her bitter dregs."

Enoch's eyes widened as visions flooded his mind - masses of people lined up at gleaming terminals, their right hands extended over scanners. "They accept the Mark willingly?"

"They believe it brings prosperity, convenience, security." Zophiel traced the shape of a beast in the dust. "The system promises peace through unity - one world, one faith, one economy. But it demands absolute allegiance."

"The green sabbath..." Enoch murmured.

"Yes. They've created a new day of rest their Sun day, mandatory cessation of commerce to 'heal the earth.' Those who refuse compliance are branded enemies of the planet." Zophiel's voice carried ancient sorrow. "The Mark becomes their passport to survival - no buying, no selling, no participation in society without it."

Enoch watched as more people materialized in his vision - crowds flowing into vast temples of glass and steel, raising their hands to screens displaying shifting symbols. "The image that speaks..."

"The marriage of religious and political power, using technology to enforce worship. Artificial intelligence becomes their oracle, predicting and controlling human behavior." Zophiel's wings trembled. "Those who resist face exclusion, persecution, death."

"And those who take the Mark?"

"They drink the full measure of divine wrath. The choice to receive the beast's name or number seals their eternal fate." Zophiel drew a line through the beast's symbol. "No redemption remains for those who pledge allegiance to this last kingdom of man."

Zophiel's wings shifted, casting a rainbow of colors across the dusty ground. "Time grows short for the two lampstands of God. Your mission, dear brother, is to help gather the last remnant - those who keep the commandments and hold fast to the faith of Yahshua."

Enoch's eyes brightened at the mention of his fellow witness. "Elijah?"

"You'll meet him soon enough." Zophiel placed a hand on Enoch's shoulder. "But first, I must ask you to stay here a while longer. The Lord has a gift for you."

"The Comforter?" Enoch's voice softened with reverence.

"Yes. The Helper, His Holy Spirit, who has dwelt among humankind these past two millennia, approaches." Zophiel gestured to the glowing meat. "While we wait, shall we share this blessing from the healing trees?"

Enoch broke off a piece of the luminescent flesh, offering it to Zophiel. The angel's face radiated joy as he accepted. They sat in comfortable silence, sharing the sacred meal as the morning sun climbed higher in the sky. Each bite filled Enoch with warmth, memories of walking along the river of healing with the Creator flooding his mind.

"This taste..." Enoch closed his eyes, savoring the flavor. "It reminds me of the fruit from the Tree of Life."

"A foretaste of what's to come." Zophiel's wings shimmered. "The leaves of healing will soon restore all nations."

A gentle breeze stirred the surrounding air, carrying the scent of rain on distant mountains. The atmosphere grew thick with anticipation as they waited for the Spirit's arrival.

As Enoch and Zophiel shared their meal, a German Shepherd emerged from behind a cluster of rocks. The dog's ribs showed through matted fur, its eyes wary yet hopeful. Despite its condition, nobility radiated from its bearing - a shadow of what animals had been in Eden.

Enoch broke off a piece of the glowing meat. The dog inched forward, nose twitching at the celestial aroma. As it accepted the morsel, Enoch's hand brushed its head, and images flooded his mind - the Garden, where lions had played with lambs, where no creature knew fear or hunger.

"If only you could have seen them then, Zophiel." Enoch's voice caught. "Before my ancestor's choice brought death to all creation."

The German Shepherd pressed against Enoch's leg, sensing his distress.

"Adam's fall." Enoch stroked the dog's fur. "One act of disobedience, and paradise crumbled. The earth itself groans under the weight of that sin. Even these innocent ones..." He gestured to the dog, now licking the last traces of meat from his fingers. "They never chose this suffering."

The morning stretched into afternoon. As the sun dipped toward the horizon, Marking the beginning of the Sabbath, the air grew heavy with presence. The camp was bathed in a light unlike Zophiel's celestial radiance. The German Shepherd's ears perked up, its eyes fixed on something unseen, and then bowed down in reverence.

A rushing wind that wasn't wind swept through the camp. Enoch felt it enter his lungs, fill his cells, transform his very essence. Power coursed through him - not the raw force of nature, but the creative energy that had spoken worlds into being. His body hummed with holy fire, his mind expanded to contain divine understanding. The Spirit of God, the same that had hovered over primordial waters, now dwelt within him.

The air crackled with divine energy as Zophiel dropped to his knees, his luminous wings wrapping around his form like a cocoon of light. The German Shepherd pressed its belly to the ground, whimpering in reverence.

Thunder rolled across the cloudless sky. The very atoms of creation seemed to pause, holding their breath in anticipation. A voice, deeper than oceans and more powerful than a thousand storms, yet gentle as a father's whisper, resonated through every particle of existence:

"This is my Lampstand, my good and faithful servant. Whom I am well pleased to call a friend. You have walked with me in the garden, and now you will receive my Mark upon you. My staff will help you guide and protect my flock."

The words carried weight beyond mere sound - each syllable contained memories of eternities past. Enoch felt them wash over him like waves of liquid light, each one bringing flashes of his walks with the Creator: discussions beneath Elysium trees, sharing wisdom beside celestial waters, witnessing the birth of stars.

The German Shepherd pressed closer to Enoch's leg, trembling not in fear but in awe of the voice that had first breathed life into its kind.

Zophiel remained bowed, his wings quivering with holy light, as the divine proclamation echoed across the barren landscape.

The voice faded, leaving behind a profound silence that seemed to vibrate with lingering power. Enoch remained on his knees, tears streaming down his face as the last echoes of divine presence settled into the earth beneath him. The ground itself had transformed - no longer mere dust and stone, but sacred soil consecrated by Jehovah's manifestation.

Zophiel rose, his wings casting prismatic light across the hallowed space. "This place is now set apart." His voice carried reverent wonder. "Like Bethel where Jacob saw the ladder, like Horeb where the bush burned, this ground will forever bear His Mark."

The angel's form shimmered, his outline blurring with celestial radiance. "Remember, Lampstand - you carry His Spirit and Staff now. Let it guide your steps." With a flash of light that turned the air into crystal, Zophiel vanished.

The German Shepherd lifted its head, watching the space where the angel had stood. Enoch remained prostrate, his lips moving in silent praise. Hours passed, the sun sank below the horizon, and stars emerged to witness his worship. Ancient psalms, songs of David, and melodies from the heavenly courts poured from his heart.

Through the night, Enoch's voice rose and fell in waves of adoration. He sang of God's majesty, of creation's beauty, of redemption's plan. The dog sat sentinel beside him, occasionally lifting its muzzle to join the songs with gentle howls.

The sacred ground seemed to pulse beneath them, as if the very atoms remembered the voice that had called them into being. Each grain of sand, each particle of dust, bore silent witness to the divine visitation that had transformed this desolate place into holy ground.

CHAPTER 3

As the Sabbath hours stretched before him, Enoch's initial awe gave way to waves of uncertainty. He paced the sacred ground, his footsteps stirring small clouds of dust. The German Shepherd watched him with attentive eyes.

"Who am I to bear such responsibility?" His fingers traced the Mark on his forehead. "Three thousand years in divine presence, yet here I stand - flesh and blood again, vulnerable to doubt."

Memories of celestial courts flickered through his mind, bright fragments that seemed to mock his current earthbound state. The weight of divine purpose pressed against his chest, threatening to crush his newly mortal frame.

The dog padded over, pressing its warm body against his leg. Enoch sank to the ground, burying his fingers in the thick fur.

"In heaven, everything was clear. The divine plan unfolded like a perfect tapestry." He gazed at the desolate landscape. "But this world... it's broken in ways I never imagined. How can one man make a difference?"

The sun crawled across the sky with agonizing slowness. Each hour of sacred rest amplified his inner turmoil. The Spirit within him burned bright, but his human vessel felt inadequate to contain such power.

"I walked with God." His voice cracked. "Now I must walk among men. What if I fail? What if this Mark, this calling, proves too heavy?"

The German Shepherd lifted its head, ears alert to something beyond human perception. Enoch felt it too - a subtle shift in the air, a reminder of the divine presence that had transformed this patch of earth. The Spirit within him stirred, not with answers, but with peace that transcended his questions.

He settled back, watching shadows lengthen across the hallowed ground. The Sabbath hours demanded patience, forcing him to sit with his doubts rather than rush into action. Perhaps that too was part of the design - this space between calling and commission, between divine touch and human response.

As the last rays of Sabbath sun faded, Enoch drifted into peaceful slumber beneath the desert stars. Rollo, the now named German shepherd curled protectively at his feet.

Dawn broke harsh and metallic. They followed the pillar. The city rose before them - a jarring maze of steel and glass that pierced the morning sky. Each step closer assaulted Enoch's senses. Vehicles screeched past, spewing fumes that burned his throat. Neon signs flickered and pulsed, their artificial glare a poor imitation of heaven's pure light.

Rollo pressed close to his leg, as confused at the noise as his master.. The weight of sin hung thick in the air, pressing against Enoch's chest like a physical force. He'd witnessed the glory of the New Jerusalem, its streets of gold and gates of pearl. This concrete jungle felt like a child's crude crayon drawing in comparison.

The Spirit within him stirred, downloading divine understanding into his mind. Modern technology, social structures, centuries of human progress - knowledge flooded his consciousness, helping him navigate this alien landscape.

They rounded a corner onto a quieter street. A massive stone church loomed ahead, its spires reaching toward heaven like grasping fingers. At its base, a man sat propped against the wall, his withered legs splayed uselessly before him. A paper cup rattled with sparse coins.

"Spare some change?" The man's eyes were dull with resignation.

Enoch knelt beside him. "Silver and gold I do not have." The Spirit surged within him, power tingling through his fingertips. "But what I have, I give you. In the name of Yahshua, the Word of God - rise and walk."

He grasped the man's hand. Divine energy crackled between them. The beggar's legs straightened, muscle and sinew knitting together before their eyes. With a cry of joy, he leaped to his feet, dancing and shouting praise. He burst through the church doors, his celebrations echoing across the stone walls.

Enoch remained outside, Rollo at his side, as curious onlookers gathered.

A man in emerald robes burst through the church doors, his face flushed with agitation. His eyes darted between the dancing beggar and the growing crowd of onlookers.

"What's all this commotion?" The priest's voice cut through the celebrations. "How are you walking?"

The beggar spun around, joy radiating from his weathered face. "That man out there, the one with the dog - he touched me and commanded me to walk in Yahshua's name. The pain vanished. My legs, they're whole again!"

The priest's expression darkened. He strode past the beggar, his green robes swishing against the stone steps. His gaze fixed on Enoch, who stood quietly beside Rollo.

"Who gave you the authority to heal on the Green Sabbath?" The priest's words carried the weight of accusation. His fingers clutched a golden medallion hanging from his neck - the symbol of his office.

Enoch raised his hands in a peaceful gesture. "God by grace alone healed this man, not by my might but by Him who is all things."

The priest's face contorted, his fingers tightening around the medallion. "Who are you to speak of such things?" His eyes narrowed as he scanned Enoch's appearance. "Where is your Mark to perform this kind of service?"

The crowd pressed closer, their whispers a rising tide of curiosity and concern. Rollo's ears flattened against his head, sensing the growing tension.

"No one shall perform miracles or work on this Green Sabbath unless they have the Mark of the Green World Church." The priest's voice carried across the gathering, drawing murmurs of agreement from several onlookers. He pulled back his sleeve, revealing a metallic emblem embedded in his flesh - a twisted tree wrapped around a globe.

The healed beggar stepped forward, his newfound strength clear in his stance. "But he healed me! I've sat on these steps for fifteen years. Now look!" He jumped again, demonstrating his restored mobility.

The priest raised his hand, silencing the man. His gaze never left Enoch, cold calculation replacing his initial anger. Behind him, two figures in matching green robes emerged from the church doors, their hands hovering near devices at their belts.

Enoch turned away from the priest, his steps measured and purposeful. Rollo matched his stride as they moved toward the town square, the growing crowd trailing behind them like a living tide. The healed beggar bounded alongside, his joy infectious despite the tension.

The square opened before them - a vast expanse of concrete and steel benches surrounding a central fountain. Digital billboards cast their artificial glow across faces both curious and cautious. Enoch climbed onto a bench, his presence drawing more onlookers from nearby shops and offices.

"People of this city," his voice carried across the square, "why do you marvel at this healing? Why do you stare as though by my own power or holiness I made this man walk?"

The crowd pressed closer. Business people with briefcases paused their hurried walks. Street vendors left their carts unattended.

"The God of Abraham, Isaac, and Jacob - the God of our ancestors - has glorified His Son Yahshua. You handed him over to death. You denied the Holy and Righteous One before the world's governments, choosing instead to embrace corruption and greed and a counterfeit religion."

Phones emerged from pockets, recording his words. The healed man stood nearby, nodding vigorously.

"You killed the Author of life, but God resurrected him.

A hush fell over the square. Even the digital advertisements seemed muted.

"Now, brothers and sisters, I know you acted in ignorance, as did your leaders who created these green laws. But God fulfilled what he had foretold through all the prophets, saying that His Christ would suffer." Enoch's voice softened with compassion. "Repent, then, and turn to God, that your sins may be wiped out, that times of refreshing may come from the Lord."

The crowd hung on his every word as he spoke of the prophets, of Moses' warnings, and of God's covenant. The afternoon sun cast long shadows across the square as he explained how all of God's promises pointed to these very days.

The priest's fingers flew across his phone's screen, his face illuminated by its glow. He whispered into the device while keeping his eyes locked on Enoch. The two robed figures behind him mirrored his actions, their movements swift and practiced.

Enoch observed their stealthy actions. The Mark on his forehead tingled - a divine warning. Rollo's ears perked up, his muscular body tensing beside his master.

A low hum filled the square as sleek vehicles with green emblems rolled to a stop at each exit. Men in tactical gear poured out, their weapons trained on the gathering.

"That's him - the unauthorized healer!" The priest's voice carried across the square. "He bears no Mark of the Green World Church!"

The crowd scattered like leaves in a storm, leaving Enoch exposed on his makeshift platform. The healed beggar stood his ground, positioning himself between Enoch and the approaching forces.

"Stand down and submit for processing." The command boomed through speakers. "Unauthorized religious activity violates Green Code 7.3."

Rollo's growl rumbled deep in his chest. Enoch placed a calming hand on the shepherd's head, even as the circle of armed men tightened around them.

"Take the dog too," the priest ordered. "All unregistered companions must be evaluated."

The tactical team advanced with practiced precision. Their boots scraped against concrete as they closed in, weapons raised. Green lasers danced across Enoch's chest.

"Final warning. Submit for processing or face immediate neutralization."

The Mark on Enoch's forehead burned brighter. Divine energy coursed through his veins, but the Spirit held him back - this was not the moment for confrontation. He raised his hands slowly, his eyes meeting the priest's triumphant gaze.

A blinding shaft of light pierced the heavens, searing through the afternoon sky like a divine blade. The tactical team staggered backward, shields raised against the impossible brightness. Their organized formation crumbled as men stumbled into each other, crying out in shock and temporary blindness.

The priest threw his arms across his face, his medallion clattering against his chest. "Don't let them escape!" His command was lost in the chaos of shouting voices and radio static.

Enoch felt Rollo's fur brush against his leg. The German Shepherd's training kicked in, guiding his master through the confusion. They slipped between the disoriented guards, their footsteps masked by the continuing commotion.

The narrow alley beckoned - a shadowy corridor between towering buildings. Enoch pressed his back against the cool brick, heart pounding as boots scraped concrete behind them. Rollo stayed low, his dark fur blending with the shadows.

"Spread out! Check every street!" The commands echoed off stone and concrete walls.

They crept deeper into the alley's embrace, past overflowing dumpsters and scattered debris. The sounds of pursuit faded, replaced by the distant wail of sirens. Rollo's ears swiveled, tracking their hunters' movements as they navigated the urban maze.

A door slammed somewhere behind them. Enoch quickened his pace, guided by the Spirit's urgent prompting. They rounded a corner just as voices carried down the passage they'd vacated.

"Clear this sector! They couldn't have gone far!"

But they had. The alley had delivered them into a maze of back streets, their pursuers' shouts now muffled by distance and the city's constant drone. The divine light that had provided their escape faded, leaving them alone in the gathering shadows of the concrete canyon.

In a dimly lit control room, screens flickered with surveillance footage from the square. Captain Sarah Reed of the Morality Division drummed her fingers against the steel desk, her other hand adjusting the green band on her uniform.

"Replay sector seven." Her eyes narrowed at the mysterious light phenomenon. "Cross-reference with known resistance tactics."

"No matches in the database, Captain." Her lieutenant swiped through data streams. "But the Las Vegas HQ wants immediate action. High Priestest Helena Vale is particularly... concerned."

The door hissed open. Captain Marcus Rivera strode in, his boots leaving wet prints on the polished floor. "The World Temple's High Priest is livid. Says this could destabilize the entire Green Sabbath system."

"One unauthorized preacher?" Reed scoffed.

"One preacher who healed a cripple without clearance or registration." Rivera tossed a tablet onto her desk. "The Church is demanding answers."

Meanwhile, three blocks away, Enoch and Rollo slipped through a rusted side door into Jose Machine Shop. Ancient lathes and drill presses loomed like sleeping giants in the shadows. The air hung thick with oil and metal shavings.

"In here." A weathered man with calloused hands ushered them behind a massive hydraulic press. "Name's Jose. The beggar you healed - he's my brother. Been praying for him for years."

Rollo sniffed the air cautiously while Enoch studied their host's face.

"Small group of us meet here." Jose wiped his hands on a rag. "Been waiting for someone like you. Someone with the true Mark."

He gestured to Enoch's forehead. "Not that green abomination they force on everyone."

Through grimy windows, emergency vehicles' lights painted the walls in alternating patterns. Jose pulled a heavy tarp over the shop's front window.

"They'll search every building eventually," Jose whispered. "But we've got a few hours. The old service tunnels under the shop - they don't know about those. Not yet."

CHAPTER 4

Jose led them through a maze of maintenance tunnels, their footsteps echoing off rusted pipes and crumbling concrete. Rust-streaked water dripped from overhead conduits, creating metallic pools on the uneven floor. The beam from Jose's ancient flashlight carved yellow swaths through the darkness.

"Watch your step here." Jose pointed to a partially collapsed section. "City forgot about these tunnels decades ago. Makes them perfect for us."

They descended three levels via a spiral maintenance staircase. The air grew thick with moisture and decay. Rollo's claws clicked against metal gratings as they crossed a narrow bridge spanning an underground stream.

The tunnel opened into a chamber roughly twenty feet square. Wooden crates served as makeshift pews, arranged in rows facing a simple wooden cross on the far wall. A few battery-powered lanterns cast warm light across the gathering space.

"This is where we worship." Jose's voice softened with reverence. "Started with just three of us. Now we're fifteen strong."

He settled onto one of the crates, shoulders heavy with untold burdens. "The Green Priests - they took control after the collapse. Saul leads them now. Claims the environmental crisis proves humanity needs strict spiritual guidance."

"But it's all about control." Jose's fingers traced the outline of a crude map scratched into the wall. "They enforce their 'Green Sabbath' - mandatory meditation sessions in their temples. Anyone caught practicing other faiths gets 're-educated.' Saul personally oversees the hunting of commandment keepers."

Jose pushes up his sleeve, revealing a network of scars. "Got these in their 're-education' center. Saul visited every day, trying to convince me the old ways were dead. That his new order was humanity's only hope."

"He's charismatic, I'll give him that. Draws crowds of thousands to the Green World Temple. But those who resist..." Jose's voice trailed off. "Let's just say many of our brothers and sisters vanished into those 're-education' centers. Never came out."

Rollo's ears perked up, head turning toward the tunnel they'd entered through. Jose immediately dimmed the lanterns.

"Patrols sometimes pass through the upper levels. We should stay quiet for a while."

The distant echo of boots filtered down from above. Enoch pressed his back against the damp wall, watching Jose extinguish the remaining lanterns. Darkness enveloped them, broken only by thin shafts of light bleeding through cracks in the ceiling.

Rollo's muscles tensed, but he remained silent - a black shape against deeper shadows. The dog's training showed in his stillness.

"Green Patrols never come down this far," Jose whispered. "But better safe than sorry."

The footsteps grew louder, accompanied by the crackle of radio static. Metal groaned overhead as the patrol crossed one of the upper bridges. Fragments of conversation drifted down.

"...sector seven clear..."

"...check the eastern junction..."

Jose touched Enoch's arm, guiding him deeper into the chamber where the wooden cross stood. The patrol's voices faded, replaced by the steady drip of water and the hollow whisper of air moving through ancient ducts.

"We can talk now." Jose relit a single lantern, keeping the flame low. The weak light caught the silver threads in his dark hair, aging him beyond his years. "But you need to understand what we're up against. Saul's got eyes everywhere - cameras, drones, informants. Above ground, they monitor everything."

He pulled a worn leather book from beneath one of the crates. The cover was scratched and water-stained, but Enoch recognized the gilt letters: Holy Bible.

"This is why they hunt us. Genuine faith - not their manufactured environmental religion. They've burned every copy they could find." Jose's fingers traced the spine with reverence. "We memorize passages, teach them to our children. When they catch someone with scriptu re..." His hand drifted to the scars on his arm.

Rollo's head snapped up, ears forward. Jose froze, hand hovering over the Bible's cover. A new sound echoed through the tunnels - the whir of mechanical servos growing closer.

The mechanical whir grew louder. Jose snatched the Bible and shoved it into a hidden compartment beneath a loose floor panel.

"Patrol droid." Jose's voice dropped to barely a whisper. "They scan for heat signatures, unauthorized gatherings."

Enoch pressed against the wall, remembering the staff the angel had given him. The smooth wood felt warm against his palm. Above them, servo motors hummed as the droid moved across the upper level.

A red beam swept down through the ceiling grates, painting crimson lines across the chamber floor. Rollo crouched low, his black fur blending into the shadows. The beam passed within inches of his paws.

Jose pointed to a narrow passage behind the wooden cross. They crept toward it, careful to avoid the searching red light. The droid paused directly overhead. Its sensors whirred, adjusting the focus.

A metallic voice crackled through its speakers. "Anomalous readings detected. Initiating deep scan."

The red beam intensified, cutting through the gloom like a knife. Enoch clutched the staff tighter, feeling the power pulse through the ancient wood. He knew what he had to do.

"Trust in Him," Enoch whispered to Jose. Before his companion could respond, Enoch stepped into the open, staff extended.

The droid's beam locked onto him. Targeting systems engaged with an electronic chirp. But as the red light touched the staff, it scattered like water hitting stone. The droid's sensors squealed, overloading from the divine energy radiating from the simple wooden staff.

Sparks erupted from the machine's joints. It spun wildly, servos grinding, before crashing through the grating. The droid smashed into the chamber floor, its red eye flickering and dying.

Jose emerged from the shadows, staring at the smoking wreck. "How did you-"

"A gift," Enoch said, lowering the staff. "From One who sees all things."

Rollo padded over to sniff the destroyed droid, his tail wagging slowly. The German Shepherd looked up at Enoch, dark eyes reflecting understanding beyond mere animal intelligence.

Enoch knelt beside the ruined droid, running his fingers across its scorched metal shell. The staff's power had left strange Markings etched into the casing - symbols that reminded him of his time beyond the veil.

"The bridegroom approaches." Enoch traced one of the symbols. "I've walked with Him, Jose. For three thousand years, I dwelt in His presence. Now He sends me with a warning - time grows short."

Jose sank onto one of the wooden crates. "Three thousand years? But that would mean-"

"I am Enoch, who walked with God and was not, for God took him." The words carried weight in the underground chamber. "Now I return as His messenger. The bride must prepare herself."

"The bride?"

"His church. His people. Those who keep His commandments and hold fast to their faith." Enoch stood, the staff gleaming in the dim light. "Gather your fifteen. Bring them here tonight. There are things they must know, preparations to be made."

Jose ran a hand through his silver-streaked hair. "Some live far from the city. The Green Patrols monitor all travel."

"The One who sent me will make a way. Go now. Tell them the bridegroom comes for His bride."

Rollo pressed against Enoch's leg, as if lending support to his words. The dog's presence seemed to steady Jose, who nodded and retrieved his flashlight.

"I'll need three hours. Maybe four." Jose paused at the tunnel entrance. "What you said about walking with God - about being Enoch - I believe you. I've seen too much today not to."

"Faith opens eyes, my friend. Go quickly."

Jose disappeared into the darkness. His footsteps faded, leaving Enoch alone with Rollo in the lantern's glow. The staff hummed softly in his grip, resonating with truths waiting to be shared.

The underground chamber filled with whispered prayers and hushed greetings as Jose's followers trickled in. They came in twos and threes, using different routes to avoid detection. Fifteen people crowded onto the wooden crates, their faces illuminated by scattered lanterns.

Enoch stood before the wooden cross, staff in hand. Rollo sat alert at his feet, watching the gathered faithful.

"Brothers and sisters," Enoch's voice carried authority born of divine presence. "I bring a message from the throne room itself. The first angel's message echoes across time: 'Fear God and give Him glory, for the hour of His judgment has come.'"

He traced symbols in the air with his staff, and they hung there glowing - ancient Hebrew letters that spelled out God's name.

"The second angel declares Babylon's fall. Your Green Priests, their environmental religion - it's all part of the great deception. They've made the earth drink from the wine of spiritual fornication."

A woman in the back row clutched her hidden Bible closer. "But what can we do? They control everything."

"The third angel's message is clear - those who worship the beast and receive his Mark face divine wrath. But those who keep God's commandments, who hold fast to their faith in Yahshua - they will stand."

Jose leaned forward. "You mentioned being a Lampstand?"

"Yes. God has sent two witnesses - myself and Elijah - to shine a light in these final days. We are the two olive trees, the two lampstands standing before the Lord of the earth."

Murmurs rippled through the group. An elderly man raised his hand. "Like in Revelation 11?"

"The very same. We come to proclaim the truth before the end. The Mark of the Beast approaches - a false sabbath, forced worship disguised as environmental protection. But God's people will receive His seal, keeping His true Sabbath holy."

The gathered believers exchanged glances, hope kindling in their eyes. Here was confirmation of what they'd suspected about the Green Priests' agenda, delivered by one who had walked with God Himself.

Enoch raised the staff, its surface catching the dim lantern light. "The time has come to leave this place. Like the Hebrews of old, you must flee to the desert."

Worried whispers rippled through the gathering. A young mother clutched her infant closer.

"But the desert's a death zone," one man protested. "The radiation storms-"

"I've come from the desert. It's safe for those who believe. The Lord, who parted the Red Sea, still reigns," Enoch's voice carried quiet authority. "As He guided His people with pillars of cloud and fire, He will guide you now."

Jose stood, his scarred arms visible in the lantern light. "When do we leave?"

"Tonight. Pack only what you can carry. The Lord will provide, just as He provided manna for our ancestors."

Rollo's ears perked up, his nose testing the air. The dog's muscles tensed, sensing the weight of the moment.

"The Green Priests and Morality police monitor all exits," Jose said. "The checkpoints-"

A soft glow filtered down through the ceiling grates - not the harsh red of patrol droids, but a gentle luminescence that filled the chamber with pearl-white light. The believers gazed upward, faces transformed by its radiance.

"There's our sign." Enoch pointed with the staff. "The pillar beckons. Gather your families. We leave within the hour."

The group dispersed quickly, moving through different tunnels to avoid detection. Soon, only Jose, Enoch, and Rollo remained in the underground chamber.

"I know a maintenance shaft that leads past the outer barriers," Jose said. "It hasn't been used in decades. The Priests won't expect anyone to go that way."

Above them, the pearly light pulsed gently, waiting to guide them into the wilderness. Enoch touched the staff to the ground, feeling divine energy flow through the ancient wood.

"Then let us go, friend. The exodus begins anew."

The remnant gathered at the maintenance shaft, their meager possessions clutched in backpacks and duffel bags. Jose pried open the rusted access panel, revealing a narrow vertical tunnel lined with ancient service ladders.

"Single file," Jose whispered. "Watch for loose rungs."

They climbed in silence, the pearl-white glow from above growing stronger with each level. Rollo followed close behind Enoch, the German Shepherd's agility defying his size as he navigated the metal steps.

At the tunnel's apex, a horizontal passage stretched toward the city's outer wall. Broken pipes and collapsed sections forced them to crawl in places. The believers helped each other through tight spots, passing children forward hand to hand.

The passage ended at a maintenance hatch. Beyond it lay the wasteland - and freedom. Jose worked the seized mechanism, muscles straining until the door cracked open with a groan.

Clean desert air rushed in. The pillar of light stood before them, a luminous column stretching from earth to sky. Its gentle radiance pushed back the darkness, creating a path through the dunes.

Enoch placed his hand on Jose's shoulder. "The Lord has chosen you to lead them."

"But I thought-"

"There are others who need to hear the message. More of God's people are trapped in different cities." Enoch lowered his head, gripping the staff with both hands as he prayed. The staff split into two, and Enoch handed one of the newly created staffs to Jose. "The pillar will guide you to safety. Make camp where it rests."

The staff hummed with power as Jose gripped it. Understanding dawned in his eyes.

"How will you find us?"

"The Spirit will direct my path." Enoch scratched Rollo behind the ears. "Keep them safe, friend."

The German Shepherd moved to Jose's side, accepting his new charge with quiet dignity.

The believers filed out into the desert night, their forms silhouetted against the pillar's glow. Jose raised the staff, and the light seemed to pulse in response.

"Go now," Enoch said. "The dawn must not find you near the city."

Jose nodded, emotion thick in his throat. He turned to follow the pillar, the remnant falling in behind him. Enoch watched until the light and his people vanished behind the dunes.

CHAPTER 5

Saul's fingers drummed against the polished bamboo desk as he reviewed the holographic arrest reports floating before him. The GWC headquarters' meditation garden outside his window stood in stark contrast to the harsh reality within.

"Bring in the first dissenter." His voice carried through the intercom.

Two guards escorted an elderly woman into his office. Her wrists bore the Marks of eco-cuffs - biodegradable restraints that would decompose within hours of removal.

"Mrs. Linbaugh. Three violations of the Green Sabbath." Saul circled her, his recycled silk robes rustling. "Operating unauthorized electronics, exceeding your weekly carbon quota, and refusing the Green Church of God Earth-Mark verification scan."

"I answer to a higher authority." Her chin lifted.

"The earth mother provides for all who follow her laws." Saul's smile didn't reach his eyes. "Yet you persist in these... primitive beliefs."

Through the one-way glass behind his desk, rows of holding cells stretched into darkness. Each contained others like Mrs. Linbaugh - believers who rejected the new order.

"The holding facilities are reaching capacity." A guard handed Saul a tablet displaying detention statistics. "The southern quadrant reports similar resistance."

Saul's fingers clenched around the tablet. "Double the patrols in sectors showing non-compliance. Increase the reward for reporting unauthorized gatherings."

"And the dissenters?"

"Transfer them to the re-education centers." Saul turned back to Mrs. Linbaugh. "The Earth mother is merciful. She offers redemption through service."

"Your false goddess has no power over me."

"Take her away." Saul waved dismissively. "Schedule her for immediate processing."

As the guards led her out, Saul activated a secure channel to the enforcement division. "Implement Protocol Omega in all residential sectors. Full surveillance, no exceptions. These believers are organizing somehow. Find their network and shut it down."

The holding cells filled with the sound of singing - ancient hymns that echoed through the detention block. Saul slammed his fist on the desk.

"Silence them!"

But the voices grew stronger, defiant in their faith. Saul stared through the glass at his prisoners, unable to comprehend their resistance to progress, to unity, to the new world they were building.

Saul strode through the underground corridors of the GWC complex, his footsteps echoing against polished stone. The latest reports burned in his mind - another healing, another miracle a disruption to their carefully maintained order.

A holoscreen flickered to life as he passed, displaying footage of the incident outside the meditation center. The beggar - a man they'd carefully placed to maintain social hierarchy - now danced through the streets, proclaiming miracles.

"Pull up all surveillance on the stranger." The command brought up fragmented images across the walls. A man in simple clothes, moving through their city with unsanctioned purpose.

His second-in-command, Ryan, fell into step beside him. "The crowd's growing. They're calling it a miracle."

"Miracles are bad for business." Saul's jaw clenched. "Where is he now?"

"Lost him in sector seven. The tracking systems... they malfunction around him."

Saul stopped at the central monitoring station. Dozens of screens showed the city's pulse - carbon credits, resource allocation, compliance scores. But sector seven remained dark.

"Send in the peacekeepers. Full sweep. I want him found."

"Sir, the people-"

"The people need structure." Saul's fingers traced the Green World Church Earth-Mark on his wrist. "This stranger threatens everything we've built. Our perfect balance."

Through the window, the city sprawled below - a testament to controlled progress. Solar towers reached toward the sky, vertical gardens cascaded down buildings, citizens moved in orderly patterns dictated by their carbon allowances.

"What about the rumors?" Ryan's voice dropped. "They say he came from-"

"Superstition." Saul cut him off. "There is no above. Only the Earth Mother, and her chosen stewards."

But doubt crept in, unwelcome and persistent. The reports described power beyond their technology, wisdom that challenged their doctrine. A threat to the carefully maintained illusion of their authority.

"Increase surveillance in the residential sectors. Monitor all gatherings. Anyone showing signs of religious deviation gets processed immediately."

The screens flickered with new alerts - more unauthorized assemblies, more whispers of miracles. Saul's carefully ordered world began to crack.

Saul paced before the GWC council chamber's floor-to-ceiling windows. The setting sun cast long shadows across the recycled bamboo floors, but the growing darkness outside couldn't match the storm brewing within him.

"The disruptions have spread to three more sectors." He pulled up a holographic map of the city. Red dots pulsed where unauthorized gatherings had been reported. "This stranger's influence grows by the hour."

The council members shifted in their chairs, their Earth-Marks glowing faintly in the dimming light.

"Perhaps we should hear him out," Councilor Wei suggested. "The people seem drawn to-"

"The people are sheep." Saul's fist crashed against the table. "They'll follow any shepherd who offers false hope."

"But the healing-"

"Staged. A ploy to undermine our authority." Saul swept his arm across the chamber. "Look what we've built. Perfect harmony with nature. Resources allocated by merit. Every citizen knowing their place."

Through the windows, the city's automated systems began their nightly shutdown. Lights dimmed in sequence, power redirected to essential services only. A model of efficiency and control.

"Deploy the drones." Saul activated the enforcement protocols. "Full spectrum surveillance. I want every corner of this city scanned."

"Sir, the privacy laws—"

"Are suspended under emergency protocols." The holograms shifted, showing thermal images of gathering crowds. "This ends tonight."

A guard burst into the chamber, face flushed. "Sir, there's been another incident. The stranger... he's teaching in the Central Plaza."

"Teaching what?" Saul's voice dropped to a dangerous whisper.

"About... about a different sabbath. Not the Green Day of Rest. He speaks of an older law."

The council chamber erupted in murmurs. Saul's fingers dug into the table's edge until his knuckles went white.

"Clear the plaza. Arrest anyone who resists. This heresy ends now."

The guard hesitated. "Sir, the peacekeepers... some of them are listening to him, too."

Saul's composure cracked. He stormed from the council chamber, his personal security detail struggling to keep pace. The elevators whisked them down to street level, where his armored transport waited.

"Take us to Central Plaza." He jabbed coordinates into the vehicle's navigation system. "Alert all loyal units to converge there."

The transport glided through streets designed for maximum efficiency, past citizens who scattered at its approach. Through the tinted windows, Saul watched his perfect world unraveling. Years of careful planning, of building a system that gave him absolute control, threatened by one man's words.

The plaza came into view. Hundreds had gathered, forming concentric circles around a simple figure who spoke without amplification, yet his voice carried clearly across the space.

"Stop here." Saul stepped out before the transport fully settled.

The crowd parted instinctively, their Earth-Marks pulsing with proximity warnings. But their eyes remained fixed on the stranger, drinking in every word.

"This is an unauthorized assembly." Saul's voice boomed through the plaza's speaker system. "Disperse immediately or face detention."

A few people shuffled away, but most stood their ground. The stranger turned, meeting Saul's gaze with calm recognition.

"Your laws chain these people to the earth." The stranger's words cut through the evening air. "But these people are meant for more."

"Arrest him." Saul signaled his guards.

But as they moved forward, their Earth-Marks flickered and died. Panic flashed across their faces - without active Marks, they couldn't access any systems, couldn't call for backup.

"What sorcery is this?" Saul's hand flew to his own Mark, still pulsing steadily.

"Not sorcery." The stranger stepped forward. "Truth. The same truth your systems try to suppress."

The crowd pressed closer, their dead Earth-Marks a silent rebellion against everything Saul had built.

"These people belong to a higher authority." The stranger's words seemed to pierce Saul's carefully constructed armor. "And no Mark of yours can change that."

A cloud materialized around Enoch, pearlescent and luminous against the plaza's stark architecture. The mist swirled outward, touching those nearest him first.

Screams erupted as the Earth-Marks reacted. Angry red welts bubbled up around the green circuitry embedded in their skin. People clutched their wrists, dropping to their knees as the blisters spread.

"My hand! It burns!" A peacekeeper collapsed, his weapon clattering across the recycled pavement.

Saul backed away, but the cloud advanced relentlessly. His guards fled, their disciplined ranks breaking as the mist reached them. Those without Marks stood unaffected, watching in horror as their Marked neighbors writhed in agony.

"Behold!" Enoch's voice carried over the chaos. "Those who have received the Mark of the Beast suffer its judgment. Your Earth-Mother is a false god, her Mark a chain upon your souls."

The cloud pulsed with divine light, exposing the true nature of the Marks. What had appeared as elegant green circuits now revealed themselves as twisted, serpentine patterns burning beneath the skin.

Saul staggered backward, clutching his wrist as the first blisters formed. His carefully maintained composure shattered as pain lanced through his arm. The Mark that had given him such power now brought him to his knees.

"What have you done to us?" Saul's voice cracked.

"I have done nothing. The truth reveals itself." Enoch stood unmoved in the center of the cloud. "Your Mark separates you from the Creator. It binds you to corruption and death."

The cloud dissipated, leaving behind a plaza filled with moaning figures. Those without Marks helped their suffering neighbors to their feet. The evening air carried the acrid smell of burned flesh and ozone.

"Your system enslaves them." Enoch approached Saul, who remained hunched over his blistered wrist. "The Mark you forced upon them corrupts body and soul."

"We brought order." Saul's voice rasped through clenched teeth. "Structure. Purpose."

"You brought chains." Enoch takes his rod and strikes the ground, sending vibrations through the recycled pavement. "The Creator gave them freedom, but you bound them to your false goddess."

Around them, people tore at their Marks, desperate to remove the burning circuits. Blood mixed with the green technology embedded in their flesh.

"The pain will pass." Enoch addressed the crowd. "But the choice remains. Your Earth-Mother demands submission through her Mark. The Creator offers freedom through faith."

"Lies!" Saul struggled to his feet, his authority crumbling like the skin around his Mark. "Without the system, there's only chaos."

"There is truth." Enoch raised his hands toward the darkening sky. "And truth breaks every chain."

The plaza's automated systems flickered and died. Screens went dark, surveillance drones dropped from the air, and the ever-present hum of technology faded to silence. For the first time in years, the people stood free from constant monitoring.

"Your Mark is a counterfeit." Enoch's words echoed across the plaza. "A perversion of the seal of God. Those who choose truth will find healing. Those who cling to lies..."

He left the warning unfinished as more people stumbled into the plaza, drawn by the commotion. Their Marks pulsed erratically, responding to the lingering presence of divine power.

Enoch turned away from the chaos in the plaza, his feet carrying him toward the city's edge. The weight of divine purpose pressed against his shoulders, heavier than the dusty pack he'd acquired. Behind him, sirens wailed through the darkening streets.

The city's outer wall loomed ahead - a marvel of sustainable architecture with its living gardens and solar panels. A guard post stood empty, its security systems dark in the wake of his presence. He passed through unhindered, stepping from recycled pavement onto raw earth.

The transition struck him physically. Each step away from the manufactured environment lifted a layer of oppression from his spirit. The artificial lights of the city faded, revealing stars that had been invisible through the pollution dome.

A cool breeze carried the scent of wild sage and desert minerals. His feet found an ancient path, worn into the rock by generations before the GWC claimed dominion. Nature's raw beauty surrounded him - untamed, unregulated, free from humanity's controlling hand.

He crested a hill as the moon rose. Below, the desert stretched endless and empty. No carbon credits needed here. No Marks to regulate movement. Just open space and the whisper of divine presence in the wind.

A natural cave opened in the hillside, offering shelter. Enoch ducked inside, leaving behind the city's distant glow. Here, in the darkness and silence, he could commune with the Creator as he had before his awakening in this strange age.

The cave's cool embrace reminded him of simpler times, when humankind looked to heaven instead of building their own gods. He settled onto the stone floor, his staff beside him, and closed his eyes.

CHAPTER 6

Emergency vehicles clogged the plaza, their green-tinted lights casting sickly shadows across the suffering masses. Medical drones hovered overhead, dispensing cooling mist onto the burns while GWC enforcement officers maintained a perimeter.

Inside the New Babylon GWC Headquarters crystal spire, High Priestess and Council Leader Helena Vale paced before the assembled emergency committee. Her and the other gathered Marks remained unblemished.

"Our scientists have isolated the compound." A researcher's hologram flickered above the conference table. "It appears to be an advanced nanotech weapon, targeting the biological components of our Marks."

"The cure?" Helena's fingers drummed against the recycled bamboo table.

"A synthetic protein sequence. It will neutralize the burning sensation and begin tissue regeneration within hours."

Screens around the chamber displayed footage from the plaza. The stranger's face appeared at multiple angles, enhanced and analyzed by AI systems.

"This terrorist used our own technology against us." Helena's voice cut through the murmurs of the committee. "Our Marks represent humanity's covenant with God and the Earth-Mother. This attack strikes at the heart of our sustainable future."

"The affected citizens report religious experiences," another councilor interjected. "Claims of divine intervention-"

"Mass hysteria." Helena waved away the concern. "A common side effect of biochemical weapons. Deploy the cure immediately. Full media coverage. Show our people that God and Earth-Mother protects her children."

Medical teams moved through the plaza, administering glowing green injections. The burns faded. Pain subsided. But fear remained etched on the faces of those who had felt their Marks turn against them.

"Find this stranger." Helena's command echoed through the chamber. "He threatens everything we've built. The harmony we've achieved. The balance with nature itself."

Surveillance drones launched into the night sky, their sensors sweeping the city's outskirts. But they found only darkness beyond the walls, and static where their signals should have reached.

Saul strode through the crystal corridors of GWC headquarters, his boots clicking against the polished floor. The Mark on his wrist throbbed - a reminder of the chaos he'd witnessed in the plaza.

The council chamber doors parted. Helena Vale stood at the head of the oval table, her silver hair caught in the glow of holographic displays.

"Report." Her fingers traced the edge of a data tablet.

"The stranger moves like a ghost." Saul planted his hands on the table. "One moment he's healing the lame, the next he's corrupting our Marks. The crowd turned into a mob of religious fanatics."

A councilman leaned forward. "Religious fanatics? We eliminated such primitive thinking decades ago."

"He speaks of an ancient deity. Claims our Marks are an abomination." Saul's jaw clenched. "The people listened. They actually listened."

Helena's eyes narrowed. "The cure is working. The physical damage can be reversed. But this ideology? This rebellion against God and Earth-Mother's guidance?"

"Permission to implement enhanced protocols." Saul straightened. "My teams can-"

"Denied." Helena circled the table. "We must maintain our image of benevolence. The people trust us because we protect them. Because we saved them from the climate wars."

"Then what do you suggest?"

"Find his followers. The ones who harbor him. Make examples of them." Helena's voice dropped. "Show them the price of betraying God and Earth-Mother's covenant. But do it quietly."

Saul nodded. The Mark on his wrist pulsed with renewed purpose. "I'll need access to the deep archives. If he's promoting ancient religions, I want to know everything about them."

"Granted." Helena waved her hand, transferring clearance codes to his neural link. "But remember - this stays within council walls. The public knows only what we tell them."

"Of course." Saul turned to leave, but Helena's voice stopped him.

"And Saul? No more public confrontations. We can't risk another plaza incident."

The holo screen flickered across the city's towers, Helena Vale's face projected a hundred feet tall against the evening sky. Her silver hair gleamed under studio lights as she addressed billions.

"Citizens of Earth, your Green World Church stands united against those who threaten our sustainable future. The terrorist known as 'the stranger' has attacked our sacred covenant with God and Earth-Mother."

Crowds gathered in the streets, their Marks glowing green in the twilight. Security drones swept searchlights across the masses.

"We offer ten million carbon credits for information leading to his capture. Those who shelter him will face immediate re-education. Remember - your Marks protect you. They connect you to Earth-Mother's blessing."

In a dimly lit control room, Saul watched multiple feeds of the announcement. His fingers traced the scars where the stranger's touch had burned his Mark.

"Deploy everything," he commanded into his neural link. "Facial recognition, thermal scanning, quantum signature tracking. I want eyes on every district."

Teams of GWC peacekeepers moved through the streets in formation, their green uniforms blending with the bioluminescent architecture. They kicked down doors, dragged suspects from their homes.

"The Green World Church embraces all religions under the faith in God and the Earth-Mother," Helena continued her broadcast. "We transcended primitive divisions long ago. This stranger seeks to drag us back to the dark ages of religious conflict."

The feeds showed detention centers filling with the accused. Some bore the Marks of healing - evidence they'd contacted the stranger. Others simply looked wrong, their social credit scores Marking them as potential sympathizers.

"Earth-Mother's love knows no bounds," Helena's voice echoed through empty alleyways. "But her justice is swift. Report any suspicious activity. Together, we will preserve the harmony we've built."

Saul's neural link buzzed with hundreds of incoming tips. The hunt had begun.

Saul's neural implant pulsed as he redirected the flood of tips to the GWC's quantum mainframe. The stream of data flickered across his enhanced vision - faces, locations, timestamps - each lead cataloged and cross-referenced against known patterns.

The elevator whispered him up to the 157th floor of the crystal spire. His office door recognized his biosignature, sliding open to reveal a wall of curved displays. The Mark on his wrist tingled as he settled into the graphene-mesh chair.

"Display courtyard incident. All angles. Full spectrum analysis."

The screens lit up with multiple perspectives. Thermal imaging showed the stranger's impossible body temperature - far below human norms. Quantum sensors revealed distortions in the fabric of local reality wherever he moved.

Saul leaned forward, studying the moment when the stranger's cloud touched the first Mark. The victim's scream came through in perfect clarity, followed by a wave of panic as others felt their own Marks burning.

But something wasn't right. He froze the frame where the stranger's hand made contact. Enhanced the image. Analyzed the light spectrum.

The Mark didn't just burn - it changed. The quantum-locked encoding that connected each citizen to the GWC's network showed signs of fundamental transformation. As if the stranger's touch rewrote the very nature of the technology.

"Cross-reference with historical religious texts," Saul commanded. The AI compiled matches - ancient accounts of divine healing, of Marks and seals, of prophets who transformed the faithful with a touch.

The footage continued. He watched himself confronting the stranger, saw his own Mark flare with pain. But now, studying the data, he noticed details he'd missed in the chaos. The stranger's eyes held recognition. As if he knew Saul. As if he saw through the layers of authority and status to something buried deep within.

Saul rubbed his scarred Mark, remembering the burning sensation. The screens filled with faces of the affected, their expressions a mix of agony and ecstasy. Whatever the stranger had done, it went beyond simple technology. It reached into the core of what the GWC had built their world upon.

Saul's fingers traced the quantum readings again, but the data defied conventional analysis. The stranger's touch hadn't just disrupted the Marks - it had altered their fundamental structure at the subatomic level. Reality itself seemed to bend around him.

The holographic displays showed molecular breakdowns of the affected Marks. Where once precise lattices of quantum-encoded information had existed, now strange patterns emerged. They resembled nothing in the GWC's vast databases - not technology, not biology, not even theoretical physics.

"Run comparison with known creation patterns."

The AI churned through petabytes of data. Natural growth sequences, cellular division, atomic bonds - everything that showed how the universe built itself. But the stranger's alterations matched none of them. They operated on principles that shouldn't exist.

Saul pulled up footage from his own encounter. Frame by frame, he watched the moment of contact. The stranger's hand hadn't just touched his Mark - it had reached through it, as if the physical world were merely a thin membrane over something vast and incomprehensible.

The quantum sensors had recorded impossible readings at the moment of contact. Space-time fluctuations that suggested the stranger's power came from outside the universe itself. Not just beyond current technology, but beyond the laws of physics that governed reality.

"Display temporal analysis."

The graphs showed time itself warping around the stranger. Not in the crude way their own time-dilation technology worked, but in smooth waves that rippled through the fabric of existence. As if he were connected to something that existed before time began.

Saul's Mark tingled with phantom pain. The scar tissue felt different under his fingers - not just damaged, but changed. As if the stranger's touch had rewritten the very atoms of his flesh with principles from beyond creation itself.

Saul drummed his fingers on his desk, the holographic displays casting a pale glow across his face. His colleague, Marcus, leaned against the doorframe, arms crossed.

"Something's been bothering me about the plaza incident." Saul pulled up the footage again. "Look at these readings."

Marcus stepped closer, his own Mark gleaming green beneath his sleeve. "What am I looking at?"

"The crowd." Saul highlighted sections of the plaza. "See these people? No reaction. No pain. No burning."

"Maybe they were out of range?"

"No." Saul shook his head. "They were right there, in the thick of it. But their biosignatures show something different - they didn't have Marks."

Marcus frowned. "That's impossible. Everyone has the Mark. It's mandatory."

"Exactly." Saul zoomed in on several faces. "Yet here they are. And whatever affected us... whatever that stranger did... it passed right through them. Like they were invisible to it."

"Could be a sensor malfunction?"

"I ran it through every analysis protocol we have." Saul's voice dropped lower. "We can't find these people in the system. No Marks, no social credits, no identity profiles. They're ghosts."

Marcus straightened, his expression hardening. "You should report this to Helena."

"Already did." Saul's fingers traced his scarred Mark. "But what if... what if the Mark isn't what we've been told? What if it's making us vulnerable to something we don't understand?"

"That's dangerous thinking, Saul." Marcus stepped back toward the door. "The Mark is Earth-Mother's blessing. It's what separates us from the wasteland savages."

"Is it?" Saul's eyes remained fixed on the screens. "Or is it what makes us controllable?"

Marcus's footsteps faded down the corridor, leaving Saul alone with his doubts. The screens still flickered with data from the plaza incident, casting shifting shadows across his office.

A notification pulsed in his neural link. Another sighting of the stranger, this time in the lower districts. The report described a gathering of unmarked individuals, sharing food and water without carbon credits or social approval.

Saul pulled up the surveillance feed. The image quality degraded at the edges, as if something interfered with the quantum sensors. Through the static, he glimpsed figures huddled in an abandoned warehouse. Their faces showed none of the vacant peace that Marked most citizens. Instead, they radiated a fierce joy, an awareness that seemed to pierce through the GWC's carefully constructed reality.

The stranger moved among them, his presence distorting the feed even further. Each time he touched someone, their Mark - if they had one - flared with that same impossible light. But unlike the plaza incident, these transformations brought no screams of pain. The people welcomed it, embraced it.

Saul's own Mark itched beneath its scar tissue. The burning sensation had never fully faded, but now it took on a different quality. Less like pain, more like... awakening.

He closed the feeds with a gesture, but not before saving the coordinates to a private server. The official response would be swift - teams of enforcers descending on the warehouse, dragging the unmarked to re-education centers. Standard procedure.

But Saul's hand hesitated over the alert button. The stranger's words from the plaza echoed in his mind: "Your Mark binds you to a false god. There is a higher truth, if you dare to seek it."

The scar tissue on his wrist pulsed, as if responding to the memory. Each heartbeat sent ripples of sensation through the quantum-encoded patterns that connected him to the GWC's network. Patterns that no longer felt as secure as they once had.

CHAPTER 7

In the dim warehouse light, Enoch watched as the Marks dissolved from their skin like morning dew. Each person's face transformed - fear and confusion giving way to wonder as the quantum-encoded patterns crumbled into dust.

"The Creator has freed you," Enoch placed his hand on a young woman's shoulder. Her tears fell onto the concrete floor where the remnants of her Mark scattered like ashes. "But this city is no longer safe for you."

"Where can we go?" An elderly man clutched his unmarked wrist. "The peacekeepers control everything."

"In the desert." Enoch's eyes held the reflection of a light beyond the physical realm. "Others await you there. Watch for the pillar. - it will guide you as it guided God's people long ago."

"A pillar?" The young woman wiped her eyes.

"Of cloud by day, of fire by night. Trust in it, as your ancestors did. The Creator provides manna each morning - you need only gather what sustains you."

The group of newly freed believers huddled closer, their faces bright with purpose despite the warehouse shadows. Enoch taught them the ancient prayers, the rhythms of worship that transcended time and space.

"Remember the Sabbath," he touched each forehead in blessing. "It is His seal, not the Mark of their false system."

Through gaps in the warehouse walls, dawn light seeped in. Enoch knew his time here had ended. The believers would need to make their own exodus now.

"Go in groups of two or three. The desert lies east of the city walls. Do not delay - the pillar will appear when you reach the wasteland's edge."

Enoch slipped out through a back entrance, leaving the converts to begin their journey. The city's massive buildings loomed overhead, their surfaces reflecting the rising sun. But his path led away from their artificial glory, back into the wilderness where heaven's light still touched the earth.

Through winding alleys and abandoned streets, Enoch made his way to the city's outskirts where a river cut through the landscape. The water's surface caught the morning light, a rare glimpse of natural beauty in this mechanized world.

The rumble of motorcycles drew his attention. Near the riverbank, a group of leather-clad bikers gathered around several people in white robes. Their bikes, adorned with crosses and biblical verses, stood in sharp contrast to their rough appearance.

A woman with silver-streaked hair stepped into the water. One biker, his beard touching his chest, raised his hands.

"In the name of Yahshua, I baptize you in the Name of the Father the Son and the Holy Ghost."

The woman emerged from the water, joy radiating from her face. She turned, catching sight of Enoch watching from the shade of a weathered oak.

"The Spirit told me you would come." She approached him, water still dripping from her clothes. "I'm Lydia. My family and I have kept the commandments, even as the Green World Church demanded our allegiance."

"You've remained faithful in difficult times." Enoch's voice carried the weight of divine authority.

"We meet in secret, preserving the true Sabbath." Lydia gestured to the bikers. "These brothers and sisters risk everything to baptize new believers. Please come to my home. We have much to discuss."

The bikers nodded respectfully at Enoch, recognition flickering in their eyes. One by one, they mounted their machines and roared away in different directions, leaving no trace of the sacred ceremony.

"Your home would be a blessing." Enoch followed Lydia along a hidden path that wound through dense undergrowth. "The Creator has preserved a remnant, even in this dark hour."

Lydia led Enoch through a maze of overgrown paths until they reached a modest house tucked behind ancient oak trees. The dwelling's exterior blended with the surrounding vegetation - a deliberate camouflage from prying eyes.

"We've converted the basement into a meeting place." Lydia pressed her palm against a weathered door. It swung open with a soft creak. "The walls are lined with lead. Blocks their scanners."

The basement revealed rows of hand-carved wooden benches facing a simple podium. Scripture verses covered the walls, written in various hands - a testament to the community's shared faith.

"My husband, Marcus, maintains our communication network." She gestured to a corner where radio equipment hummed quietly. "We coordinate with other believers across the west coast."

A teenage boy emerged from behind the equipment, his eyes widening at the sight of Enoch. "The cloud appeared again this morning. East of the city."

"Joshua keeps watch for signs." Lydia squeezed her son's shoulder. "He's young, but his faith runs deep."

"The pillar guides those who seek truth." Enoch traced his fingers along the nearest scripture verse. "How many gather here?"

"Twenty families, sometimes more." Lydia's voice dropped. "We rotate meeting times, never the same pattern. The peacekeepers have gotten better at tracking large groups."

Joshua adjusted a dial on the radio, and static-filled voices filtered through the speakers. "Another group broke free from the re-education camp. They're heading for the desert."

"The Spirit moves like wind through the city." Enoch closed his eyes, sensing the invisible currents of divine purpose. "More will follow."

"We've prepared supplies." Lydia opened a hidden panel on the floor, revealing caches of water and preserved food. "For those who choose to flee."

The radio crackled again. A voice cut through the static: "Enforcement squads mobilizing. Southeast sector. Multiple targets."

Joshua's fingers flew across the equipment. "That's near the river. Where the baptisms were."

"They're getting closer." Lydia's face tightened with concern. "We need to warn the others."

Enoch moved swiftly to the radio equipment, placing his hand on Joshua's shoulder. The boy shifted aside, allowing him access to the controls.

"The frequency." Enoch's fingers hovered over the dials. "What channel reaches the desert camps?"

"Here." Joshua adjusted a switch, and the static cleared. "But the enforcers monitor everything now."

Enoch leaned toward the microphone. His voice carried the same authority that had once moved mountains. "To all who hear: The hour grows late. The serpent's teeth seek those who gathered at the river. Move east. The pillar awaits."

He spoke in the ancient tongue, words that flowed like water over stones. The message complete, he stepped back from the equipment.

"They'll understand?" Lydia clutched a worn Bible to her chest.

"Those meant to hear will know." Enoch turned his attention to the basement's layout. "Your sanctuary needs stronger protection."

He retrieved the rod from his cloak. Its surface caught the dim light, revealing symbols carved into the ancient wood. Enoch touched it to each corner of the room, and the air shifted. A presence settled over the space, invisible but tangible.

"What did you do?" Joshua's eyes widened as he sensed the change.

"The same protection that guarded the ark." Enoch returned the rod to his cloak. "No evil can pierce these walls now."

The radio crackled again. Different voices now - harsh commands and the sound of vehicles moving through streets.

"They're setting up checkpoints." Joshua's hands clenched into fists. "Scanning for Marks."

"Or lack of them." Lydia moved to a shelf, began pulling out blankets and supplies. "We need to get word to the others. Not everyone made it to the desert."

"The time for hiding draws to a close." Enoch watched as mother and son worked with practiced efficiency, preparing for whatever came next. "The Creator calls His people into the open."

Lydia's fingers worked swiftly, packing emergency supplies into weathered backpacks while Joshua monitored the radio frequencies.

The basement hummed with tense energy beneath the protection Enoch had established.

"Three more checkpoints activated." Joshua adjusted his headphones. "They're using the new quantum scanners."

A sharp knock echoed from above. Lydia froze, her hand hovering over a stack of blankets. Three more knocks followed in rapid succession.

"The signal." She exhaled. "Marcus."

Joshua bounded up the stairs, unlocking the series of bolts. Marcus burst through, his maintenance uniform stained with grease and sweat.

"They're converting the old stadium into a processing center." Marcus pulled off his work gloves. "Installing Mark stations at every entrance. Anyone without it gets sent straight to re-education."

"The temple of their false god." Enoch's voice carried across the basement.

Marcus startled, noticing their visitor for the first time. He dropped to one knee, recognition flooding his features. "The cloud - it was you."

"Rise, brother." Enoch gestured for Marcus to stand. "What else did you witness?"

"They're scared." Marcus joined them near the radio equipment. "The Marks keep dissolving, no matter how many times they reapply them. The quantum pattern won't hold."

"Their technology cannot override divine authority." Enoch traced the ancient symbols carved into his rod. "The Creator's seal claims His people."

The radio crackled with new transmissions - enforcer units coordinating their search patterns through the city. Joshua's hands flew over the dials, tracking their movements.

"They're pushing east." Joshua pointed to a crude map pinned to the wall. "Trying to cut off the escape routes to the desert."

"But they can't see the pillar." Lydia smiled, hope lighting her eyes. "Only those meant to follow it."

Marcus pulled a data chip from his pocket. "Downloaded their patrol schedules. Next shift change is in two hours."

"Then we have work to do." Enoch moved toward the supplies Lydia had gathered. "More will seek freedom before nightfall."

Enoch and Marcus worked swiftly, transferring supplies into weathered backpacks while Joshua monitored the radio frequencies. The basement thrummed with purpose beneath the divine protection.

"Southeast corridor clear." Joshua adjusted his headphones. "Three minutes until the next patrol."

Marcus spread the data chip's contents across a battered tablet. "They've doubled the quantum scanners at each checkpoint. But look-" He pointed to a gap in the coverage. "The old maintenance tunnels. They run straight through to the eastern quarter."

"The ancient paths remain." Enoch traced his finger along the tunnel route. "As it was in the catacombs."

Lydia emerged from a hidden alcove carrying bottles of water. "These tunnels - they're not on the peacekeepers' grid?"

"Officially condemned." Marcus tucked the tablet away. "But I've kept them clear. Just in case."

A burst of static cut through the radio's steady hum. Joshua leaned forward, adjusting frequencies with practiced precision. Through the white noise, a voice emerged:

"...group of seven... no Marks detected... heading toward checkpoint four..."

"That's Rachel's family." Lydia gripped the edge of the radio desk. "They were at the river this morning."

"The tunnels intersect near their location." Marcus grabbed a duffle bag full of supplies. "If we move now-"

"No." Enoch placed his hand on Marcus's shoulder. "Your role lies here, coordinating the escape routes." He retrieved his rod from beneath his cloak. "I will guide them."

"But the peacekeepers-" Lydia started.

"Cannot see what the Creator conceals." Enoch's eyes held the reflection of divine authority. "The same power that dissolves their Marks will shield His people."

Joshua's fingers flew across the radio dials. "Checkpoint four deploying additional units. They're closing the net."

"Time grows short." Enoch moved toward the basement steps. "Keep monitoring the frequencies. When you hear the thunder, direct the others to the tunnels."

"Thunder?" Joshua looked up from his equipment. "The forecast is clear."

"Not all storms come from the sky." Enoch ascended the stairs, his rod gleaming with ancient symbols in the dim light.

Enoch moved through the city's shadows, his steps guided by a wisdom beyond mortal understanding. The rod in his hand pulsed with divine energy, responding to the quantum scanners that swept the streets in regular patterns.

A group of enforcers passed nearby, their boots clicking against the cracked pavement. Their wrist-mounted devices cast green light across building facades, searching for unauthorized citizens. Enoch pressed against a wall, but not out of fear - the scanners' beams bent around him like water around a stone.

Through winding alleys and past abandoned storefronts, he tracked Rachel's family. Their fear left traces only he could perceive, a trail of desperate prayer rising above the city's mechanical hum.

He found them huddled behind a dumpster, three children clutching their parents' hands while two elderly couples kept watch. Their faces bore the peace of recent baptism despite their circumstances.

"The Creator sent you," Rachel whispered, recognition flooding her features.

Enoch touched his rod to the ground. The pavement rippled, revealing the entrance to a maintenance tunnel that had been sealed for decades.

"The ancient path awaits." He gestured toward the opening. "The peacekeepers cannot follow where He leads."

The sound of boots and scanner beeps grew closer. Rachel's youngest daughter whimpered, but Enoch placed his hand on her head.

"Fear not, little one. The same power that parted the sea guides us now."

One by one, they descended into the tunnel. Enoch followed last, sealing the entrance behind them. In the darkness, his rod's symbols cast enough light to illuminate their path - a modern echo of the pillar that had led Israel through the wilderness.

Above them, peacekeepers' boots marched past their hidden route. But in the depths of the city, guided by divine wisdom, Rachel's family moved steadily toward freedom.

Through the maintenance tunnel's darkness, Enoch's rod cast a soft glow that illuminated their path. The ancient symbols carved into its surface pulsed with each step, responding to the quantum scanners that hummed overhead.

Rachel's youngest daughter stumbled over a broken pipe. Her brother caught her arm before she fell.

"Watch your step, Sarah." Rachel steadied both children. "The path isn't smooth."

Water dripped from rusted pipes above, creating a rhythm that masked their footsteps. The tunnel walls bore the Marks of decades of neglect - crumbling concrete and exposed rebar that spoke of a civilization's decay.

"The peacekeepers' scanners can't penetrate these depths?" One of the elderly men, his voice barely above a whisper.

"Their technology fails where divine protection stands." Enoch touched his rod to a junction in the tunnel. Ancient symbols flared briefly, showing their route. "Left here. The eastern quarter lies ahead."

The group moved carefully through the darkness, their breathing steady despite the stale air. Above them, the city's mechanical heart beat continued - GWC patrols and quantum scanners searching for those who refused the Mark.

Sarah clutched her mother's hand tighter as distant boots echoed through a ventilation shaft. The rod's light dimmed automatically, leaving them in near-total darkness until the patrol passed.

"How much further?" Rachel's husband adjusted his grip on their supply pack.

"The desert's edge waits beyond the next junction." Enoch paused, sensing the currents of divine guidance. "The pillar will appear when we emerge."

The tunnel's atmosphere shifted - fresher air flowed from ahead, carrying the scent of open spaces. The rod's symbols brightened, revealing a maintenance ladder that led upward toward a sealed hatch.

Enoch placed his hand on the hatch's rusted surface. Ancient symbols flowed from his rod, tracing patterns across the metal. The seal cracked with a soft hiss, decades of corrosion falling away.

"Wait here." He ascended the ladder, each rung groaning under his weight.

The hatch opened to a loading dock behind an abandoned warehouse. The eastern sky glowed with approaching dawn, but another light caught his attention - a familiar pillar of cloud hovering just beyond the city's edge.

Enoch scanned the area. No GWC patrols in sight. The quantum scanners' green beams swept past several blocks away, focused on the main thoroughfares. He returned to the tunnel entrance.

"The way is clear." He helped Sarah up first, then assisted the others as they emerged one by one.

Rachel gasped as she saw the pillar. "Just like in the ancient stories."

"The Creator's guidance never changes." Enoch sealed the hatch behind them, the symbols fading back into ordinary rust. "Though the world forgets, His methods remain."

The group moved between empty buildings, staying close to the shadows. Looming ahead, the city's edge Marked a stark boundary between urban decay and open desert. The quantum scanner network ended at the last row of structures, creating a dead zone where the peacekeepers rarely ventured.

Sarah pointed to the pillar, her eyes wide. "It's moving."

The cloud shifted eastward, leading them toward freedom. Behind them, the city's mechanical hum faded, replaced by the whisper of desert wind.

"Others will follow," Enoch said, watching the pillar's steady progress. "The Creator calls His people from every corner."

CHAPTER 8

The desert camp sprawled across the valley floor, a patchwork of tents and simple structures that housed the growing remnant. Where once fifteen souls had huddled around a single fire, now over fifteen hundred gathered in circles of community that spread outward like ripples in still water.

Enoch walked among them, his rod casting gentle light in the pre-dawn darkness. Children darted between tents, their laughter a stark contrast to the fearful silence they'd known in the cities. The aroma of fresh manna filled the air - each morning's miracle that sustained their growing numbers.

"The latest group arrived last night." Jose fell into step beside him. He direct Rachel and her family now part of a larger extended family. "Three hundred more, led through the tunnels by Marcus."

A group of elders gathered near the central meeting area, their faces illuminated by lamplight. They rose as Enoch approached.

"The enforcers have doubled the patrols." Marcus pointed toward the distant city lights. "But their scanners still can't detect the tunnel network."

"The Creator's ways remain hidden from those who trust in machines." Enoch touched his rod to the ground, and symbols spread across the sand in a living map of the region. "New routes appear as needed."

Around them, the camp stirred to full wakefulness. Those who'd kept night watch greeted those emerging for morning prayers. The pillar of cloud that had led them here remained steady above the camp, a constant reminder of divine protection.

"We'll need to expand the water collection system." An elder gestured to where children filled containers from springs that had burst forth from the desert floor. "The Creator provides, but we must be wise stewards."

Voices lifted in morning song drifted across the camp - ancient hymns mixed with new melodies born from their desert exile. The sound echoed off the canyon walls, carrying hope instead of fear.

Jose, now the leader of this remnant church embraces the desert living, helped distribute the morning's manna to recent arrivals. "Like Moses and the Israelites," he explained to wide-eyed children. "God's provision hasn't changed." The day's activities bore witness to the Love of God, that each man should love his neighbor as himself.

***

The leaders huddled closer as night descended, their whispers carrying traces of fear. Sarah, a remnant leader, clutched her worn Bible, knuckles white. Marcus paced, his eyes darting to the distant city lights. Even Jose's usual steady demeanor showed cracks of concern.

"The GWC's drones grow bolder each day." Marcus pointed to the sky. "They'll find us soon."

"Our caves won't hide us forever." Sarah's voice trembled. "The thermal scanners-"

Enoch planted his rod in the desert sand, its light pulsing with a gentle rhythm. "You see with earthly eyes, my friends." He knelt in the dirt, hands raised to the star-filled heavens. "Father, show them what you've shown me. Open their eyes to Your protection."

The air shifted. A cool breeze swept through the camp, carrying the scent of lightning and rain. The leaders gasped as their vision transformed. The desert night blazed with holy light.

Angels stood rank upon rank, their armor gleaming with celestial fire. They filled the valleys and crowned the mountain peaks, warriors of light stretching beyond mortal sight. Their wings spread like shields of burnished gold, their sword's flames of living light.

"Ten thousand times ten thousand," Jose breathed, falling to his knees.

Sarah wept, her Bible pressed to her chest. "They've been here all along."

The angelic host towered above the camp, their presence both terrible and beautiful. Some stood as sentinels, others moved in complex patterns of celestial guardianship. Their faces shone with divine purpose, eyes like stars watching in every direction.

Marcus stopped his pacing, trembling. "The GWC's weapons... they're nothing compared to this."

"Now you understand." Enoch's rod pulsed in harmony with the angelic light. "We've never been alone in this desert. The Father's protection surrounds us, just as it did the prophets of old."

The leaders stood in awe, their fears transformed by the vision of heaven's army. Their mortal concerns about drones and thermal scanners seemed small against the backdrop of divine protection.

The vision faded, but its impact remained etched on the leaders' faces. Jose pulled a worn map from his pocket and spread it across a flat rock, his fingers tracing the routes they'd established.

"The eastern passage brought in fifty more last night." He circled a section with his finger. "Most of them factory workers who refused the Mark."

Enoch knelt beside the map, his rod casting soft light across its surface. The parchment transformed beneath its glow, revealing hidden paths that hadn't existed moments before.

"Here." He touched a spot where mountains met desert. "The Creator has prepared new ways."

Sarah leaned forward, her eyes widening at the revelation. "Those cliffs were impassable yesterday."

"Nothing is impassable to the Most High." Enoch stood, brushing sand from his cloak. "The same power that parted the Red Sea shapes these rocks to His purpose."

The camp stirred with morning activity. Children gathered fallen manna, their baskets filling with heaven's bread. Others drew water from springs that defied the desert's harsh climate. Songs of praise mixed with the sounds of life - tools at work, children at play, prayers lifted in gratitude.

Marcus returned from his patrol, dust coating his clothes. "Three more groups approach from the north. They speak of increased persecution in the cities. The GWC's enforcers conduct house-to-house searches now."

"The Father knows His own." Enoch's voice carried peace despite the troubling news. "Not one of His children will be lost to the enemy's deception."

A young girl ran past, stopping to show Enoch her basket of manna. Her eyes sparkled with joy untouched by the world's darkness. "Look! It tastes like honey today!"

Enoch smiled, remembering ancient days when other children had made the same discovery in another desert. Some truths remained constant through all ages - God's provision, His protection, His presence among His people.

* * *

The morning sun cast long shadows across the desert camp. Enoch gathered the remnant leaders near the central fire, his rod glowing with an otherworldly light.

"My time here draws to a close." His words fell heavy on the circle of faithful. "The Spirit calls me to the eastern cities."

Sarah clutched her Bible closer. "But we need your guidance, your wisdom-"

"You have something greater." Enoch pointed to her worn scriptures. "The Father's words light your path. His Spirit dwells within each of you."

Jose stepped forward, his weathered face etched with concern. "The eastern cities are death traps. GWC enforcers control every street."

"Where the darkness runs deepest, His light must shine brightest." Enoch planted his rod in the sand. "Others await, lost sheep seeking truth amid the world's lies."

Marcus bowed his head. "When will you return?"

"The Spirit leads where He wills." Enoch embraced each leader. "Your faith has grown strong. Continue in what you've learned."

The morning breeze stirred, carrying the scent of desert flowers. Enoch raised his hands in blessing over the gathered remnant. His form shimmered like heat waves rising from sun-baked sand.

"Remember-" His voice seemed to come from everywhere and nowhere. "The Father never abandons His children."

In the space between one heartbeat and the next, Enoch vanished. The desert air rippled where he had stood. Only his boot prints remained in the sand.

The remnant leaders stood in stunned silence, staring at the space where their teacher had been. Only the morning wind moved, carrying the distant sound of children gathering manna, unaware that their guardian had departed.

***

The neon lights of Paradise Casino pierced the night. Enoch walked past rows of slot machines, their electronic chimes a discordant symphony. A crowd gathered near the sports betting counter, surrounding a young woman perched on a velvet throne.

"The Ravens by fourteen points." Her voice carried an unnatural echo. "Bet your life savings. I've never been wrong."

The crowd surged forward, waving credit chips. Behind the girl, a man in an expensive suit smiled, counting his profits.

"Your demon speaks false hope." Enoch stepped through the crowd.

With a snap of her head, the girl turned toward him, her eyes solid black. "The walker between worlds. The one who dwells in light."

The casino owner moved between them. "Back off, stranger. She's my property."

"No soul belongs to you." Enoch raised his hand. "In Yahshua's name, leave her."

The girl convulsed, her throne toppling. A shriek tore from her throat - inhuman, ancient. She collapsed, color returning to her face.

The owner's face twisted with rage. "Security! This man attacked my employee!"

GWC enforcers materialized from the shadows, their green armbands glowing. They grabbed Enoch's arms.

"You're under arrest for assault and disrupting commerce." The lead enforcer pressed his shock baton against Enoch's ribs. "Take him to containment."

They dragged him through underground tunnels to a holding cell. The steel door clanged shut, leaving him in darkness.

"Another religious fanatic." The guard spat. "Enjoy your re-education."

Enoch sat on the concrete floor. Peace filled him despite his circumstances. He sang ancient psalms, his voice carrying through the cellblock.

Other voices joined him, hesitant at first, then growing stronger. Prisoners in nearby cells added their voices to the forbidden songs of praise.

The guards shouted threats, but the singing continued, echoing off steel and concrete, transforming the prison into a sanctuary of worship.

The ground rumbled. Concrete dust rained from the ceiling as the first tremors shook the prison complex. The singing stopped, replaced by shouts of alarm.

Metal groaned. The cell doors rattled in their frames. A crack split the floor, zigzagging between Enoch's feet.

"Everyone stay calm!" A guard's voice cracked with panic. "This is a standard seismic event-"

The lights flickered and died. Emergency sirens wailed through the darkness. Another violent shake sent prisoners stumbling into walls.

"The doors!" someone shouted. "They're opening!"

The electronic locks failed as backup power systems overloaded. Cell doors slid open with hydraulic hisses. Confused prisoners spilled into the corridors.

Enoch stood, steadying himself against the wall. The crack in his cell had widened into a fissure. Steam rose from its depths, carrying the scent of sulfur.

Guards scrambled to maintain control, but the quake intensified. Support beams buckled. Chunks of ceiling crashed onto the prison floor.

"This way!" Enoch's voice cut through the chaos. "Follow the emergency lights!"

Prisoners and guards alike turned toward his voice. Another violent shake knocked them off their feet. Water pipes burst, spraying corridors with scalding steam.

The fissure in Enoch's cell spread, consuming entire sections of the floor. Deep rumbling echoed from below, like the earth itself was groaning.

"The building's coming down!" A guard dropped his shock baton, abandoning his post. "Everyone out!"

The quake peaked. Walls crumbled. Support columns snapped like twigs. The prison complex collapsed in on itself, swallowed by the widening chasm.

Enoch lunged through the steam, grabbing a guard who stumbled near the growing fissure. The man's green armband flickered in the emergency lights.

"Let me go!" The guard thrashed against Enoch's grip.

"Your life matters more than your pride." Enoch pulled him away from the crumbling edge. "Help me get the others out."

Chunks of concrete rained around them. The guard stared at Enoch, recognition dawning in his eyes. "You're the one they're hunting-"

"Direct them to the service tunnel." Enoch pressed the guard's dropped shock baton back into his hands. "You know the way."

The guard hesitated, then nodded. He raised his voice over the rumbling. "Service tunnel! This way!"

Enoch spotted an elderly prisoner trapped beneath fallen debris. He braced his shoulder against the concrete slab, muscles straining. The old man crawled free, blood streaming from a gash in his forehead.

"Can you walk?" Enoch supported the man's weight.

"I think so-" The prisoner's legs buckled.

The guard returned, slinging the old man's other arm over his shoulder. "The tunnel's thirty meters ahead. Most made it through."

They half-carried, half-dragged the injured prisoner through corridors filling with smoke and steam. Other stragglers stumbled past, following the guard's directions.

A woman's scream echoed from a side passage. Enoch passed his burden fully to the guard. "Get him out. I'll find her."

"You'll die in here!"

"Go!" Enoch disappeared into the smoke.

The guard watched him vanish, then continued toward safety, supporting the old man through the chaos of the collapsing prison.

Through the smoke-filled corridor, Enoch followed the screams. Fallen debris blocked his path, forcing him to climb over twisted metal and shattered concrete. The emergency lights flickered, casting strange shadows through the steam.

"Help! Please!" The woman's voice came from behind a partially collapsed wall.

Enoch squeezed through a narrow gap. A young prisoner lay pinned beneath a fallen support beam, her GWC uniform Marking her as a guard rather than an inmate.

"Hold still." Enoch knelt beside her. Blood soaked through her sleeve where the beam had trapped her arm.

"I can't feel my fingers." Tears cut tracks through the dust on her face. "Everyone ran-"

The floor shuddered. More concrete crashed down around them. Enoch braced himself against the beam, muscles straining as he tried to lift it.

"It's too heavy." The guard's voice cracked. "Save yourself."

"The Father's strength flows through all things." Enoch closed his eyes, remembering the divine presence he'd known for three millennia. Power surged through him - not his own, but a gift freely given.

The beam shifted. The guard pulled her arm free, gasping as the circulation returned. Enoch helped her stand, supporting her weight as they navigated the destruction.

"Why?" She stumbled against him. "You're the one we were hunting. The terrorist-"

"Labels mean nothing." Enoch guided her around a fallen ceiling panel. "Only actions reveal truth."

They emerged into the main corridor. Smoke burned their lungs. The service tunnel entrance glowed ahead like a beacon in the chaos.

"Almost there." Enoch quickened their pace as the rumbling intensified. "The Father provides a way-"

The ceiling gave way behind them. A wave of dust and debris chased them down the corridor. They dove through the service tunnel entrance as the prison collapsed completely.

In the relative safety of the tunnel, the guard slumped against the wall, cradling her injured arm. "I don't even know your name."

"Names matter less than choices." Enoch touched her shoulder. Divine energy flowed through his fingers, mending torn flesh and broken bone. "Choose truth over comfort. Life over death."

He stepped back as other guards approached with medical supplies. The young woman stared at her healed arm, then at the stranger who had saved her.

But Enoch had already vanished into the shadows of the tunnel, following the Spirit's call to his next task.

The neon-drenched Paradise City square buzzed with panic. Emergency vehicles wailed past broken storefronts. Crowds gathered around portable screens broadcasting footage of the collapsed prison.

Enoch materialized atop the central fountain, his form solidifying like morning mist condensing into flesh. The water ceased flowing, glass-smooth and mirror-still beneath his feet.

"People of Paradise City!" His voice carried across the square without effort. "You witnessed the earth shake and foundations crumble. Yet you cannot see the greater tremors approaching."

Heads turned. Phones raised to record him. GWC peacekeepers pushed through the growing crowd.

"Your temples of chance and pleasure stand empty while souls starve. You wear the Mark of false salvation while rejecting divine truth." He pointed to a man's glowing green armband. "These chains you chose bind tighter than prison walls."

"It's him - the terrorist!" Someone shouted. But no one moved to stop him.

"The earthquake freed bodies, but who will free your spirits? The Father's commands bring life, not the empty promises of men. His Sabbath rest awaits while you chase digital dreams."

A peacekeeper raised his weapon. "Stand down and surrender!"

"Your bullets cannot stop the truth." Enoch spread his arms. "The Way stands open - not through neon gates or Marked wrists, but through humble obedience to eternal law. Choose this day whom you will serve."

The fountain water rose around him in crystalline sheets, refracting rainbow light across the square. Those nearest felt drops fall on their faces - not water, but tears of pure compassion.

"The time of choice grows short. Return to the ancient paths. Keep the Father's commands. Rest in His Sabbath. The Mark you wear leads to destruction, but His seal brings life."

The fountain water cascaded down in sheets, drenching the crowd. People gasped as their green armbands flickered, some failing completely.

"Arrest him!" The lead peacekeeper's command crackled through radio static. A dozen officers converged on the fountain.

"Your technology fails." Enoch's voice remained calm. "But His word endures forever."

Jose pushed through the crowd, his face hidden beneath a worn hood. He pressed something into the hands of those whose Marks had failed - small silver coins gleaming with ancient symbols.

"The old ways still live." Jose's whisper carried to those nearby. "Trade these in the shadow markets. Stay free of their system."

More armbands winked out across the square. Panic rippled through the crowd as payment systems crashed. Store security gates slammed shut, trapping shoppers inside.

"This is your doing!" A peacekeeper aimed his weapon at Enoch. "Shut down the fountain!"

"I merely reveal what already exists." Enoch stepped down from the fountain's edge. The water returned to normal, but those touched by it felt changed - lighter, as if invisible chains had fallen away.

Sirens wailed closer. Armored vehicles pushed through the gathering crowd. GWC elite forces deployed in tactical formation, their weapons trained on the fountain.

"Your last chance, terrorist." The squad commander's voice boomed through amplifiers. "Surrender, or we open fire."

Jose slipped another coin to a trembling woman whose Mark had failed. "Remember the Sabbath," he whispered. "Find us in the desert when you're ready."

The crowd shifted, creating a space between Enoch and the GWC forces. The fountain's surface rippled, though no wind blew.

"Truth cannot be captured." Enoch's form blurred at the edges. "Nor can light be imprisoned by darkness."

The elite squad opened fire. Bullets passed through empty air as Enoch vanished like morning mist burned away by the sun. Only his words remained, echoing across the square:

"Choose this day..."

CHAPTER 9

In his private chambers atop the GWC headquarters, Saul paced before a wall of screens displaying surveillance footage from Paradise city square. He paused the feed on Enoch's face, studying the stranger's features with cold calculation.

"Find me our best infiltrators." He pressed a button on his desk. "The ones who haven't taken the Mark."

Two figures entered his office minutes later. Their plain clothes and unremarkable faces made them perfect for blending into any crowd. No green bands glowed on their wrists or foreheads.

"The remnant groups are growing." Saul's fingers traced the edge of his desk. "This stranger's appearance has sparked a movement. People are abandoning the Mark, trading in silver coins, gathering in the desert."

He turned to face the agents. "I need eyes and ears among them. Learn their ways, gain their trust, find their weaknesses."

"What about the Mark?" The female agent held up her bare wrist. "They'll know we're GWC if we've taken it."

"That's why I chose you." Saul grinned in a deceiving smile. "You're my clean ones. The ones I kept pure for moments like this. They'll believe you're seeking truth, fleeing our system."

He handed each agent a small pouch of silver coins. "Use these to establish credibility. Learn their meeting places, their leaders, their plans."

"And the stranger?" The male agent weighed the coins in his palm.

"Find out where he appears next. What powers he possesses. His connection to these..." Saul waved at a screen showing the mysterious cloud. "Events."

The agents nodded, understanding their mission.

"Remember - these people believe they follow divine law. Mirror their convictions. Speak their language. Become one of them." Saul's voice hardened. "Then tear them apart from within."

The desert sun beat down as Asher and Selene trudged behind a group of Mark-less believers. Their feet sank into loose sand with each step, slowing their progress. The other travelers moved with purpose, their eyes fixed on something ahead that the two infiltrators couldn't see.

"They're following nothing." Asher wiped the sweat from his brow. "Just walking blind into the wasteland."

Selene adjusted her headscarf, scanning the horizon. "Saul said they claim to follow some kind of pillar. Like their ancient stories."

The group ahead maintained a steady pace despite the harsh conditions. Their water supplies should have run low hours ago, yet they pressed on without stopping to rest or drink.

"Something's wrong." Asher grabbed Selene's arm. "Look at their water skins - still full after six hours in this heat."

A young woman dropped back from the main group, falling in step beside them. "You seem troubled, friends. Is the journey too difficult?"

"No, just..." Selene forced a smile. "We're not used to desert travel."

"The Lord provides." The woman offered her water skin. "Like He did for our ancestors."

Asher took a careful sip, eyes widening at the cool, sweet taste. The water felt alive somehow, refreshing more than quenching thirst.

The main group began to sing hymns as they walked, their voices carrying across the dunes. Songs about deliverance, about following divine guidance through wilderness places.

"How much further?" Asher asked between verses.

"The pillar will lead us there." The woman pointed ahead at the empty air. "Just as it led us out of Paradise City."

Selene exchanged a glance with her partner. These people moved with absolute conviction, following something invisible to their eyes. Either they were all delusional from heat and religious fervor, or...

The singing grew louder as the group crested another dune. Their voices echoed with joy and purpose while Asher and Selene struggled to keep pace, blind to whatever sign guided their path deeper into the desert.

The group wound through narrow mountain passes, their path hidden between towering rock walls. Shadows deepened as the sun struggled to reach the canyon floor. No roads or trails marked these passages. - they seemed to materialize before the believers while remaining invisible to Asher and Selene.

"These canyons aren't on any maps," Asher whispered, his hand trailing along the rough stone surface. "GWC surveillance should have spotted gatherings out here."

The woman who'd shared her water walked beside them, her steps confident despite the treacherous terrain. "The Lord conceals what He wishes to protect."

The canyon twisted left, then right, opening into broader passages before narrowing again. Rock walls rose hundreds of feet overhead, their layers telling ancient stories in bands of red and gold. The air grew cooler as they descended deeper into the mountain's embrace.

A child's laughter echoed off the stone walls. The sound bounced and multiplied until it seemed to come from every direction. The group rounded another bend, and the canyon opened into a vast natural amphitheater. Tents dotted the landscape, their fabric a patchwork of earth tones that blended with the surrounding rock. People moved between the dwellings, carrying water, preparing food, teaching children.

"Welcome to the camp," their guide smiled, gesturing at the hidden community. "Here, we keep the commandments and wait for Yahshua return."

Smoke rose from cooking fires, carrying the scent of fresh bread. Gardens grew in terraced plots where the canyon walls received the most sunlight. Children played near a clear stream that cut through the center of the settlement.

Asher counted at least two hundred tents, with more tucked into natural alcoves in the rock walls. The remnant had built something remarkable here, hidden from the world's eyes.

"How many?" Selene asked, trying to keep the tension from her voice.

"More arrive each day." Their guide pointed to a group setting up new shelters. "The Lord sends those who seek truth."

The guide led Asher and Selene through the winding paths between tents toward a large cavern mouth in the canyon wall. Cool air drifted from the natural storage space, carrying the scent of dried herbs and preserved food.

"We call this New Eden." The woman gestured at the organized rows of supplies. Wooden crates held fresh vegetables, while dried goods hung in neat bundles from the ceiling. Handmade pottery lined stone shelves carved into the rock walls, each vessel labeled with its contents.

"Take what you need, leave what you can - we share everything here." She picked up an empty basket and handed it to Selene. "The Lord provides through our combined efforts."

Asher examined the careful organization. No electronic inventory systems or security measures protected these resources. Simple paper lists tracked quantities and needs.

"How do you prevent people from taking too much?" He ran his fingers over a jar of preserved fruit.

"We don't." The guide smiled. "Greed loses its power when everyone's needs are met," the guide smiled

A young boy darted into the cavern, depositing a basket of fresh-picked herbs on one of the tables. He grinned at the newcomers before racing back outside to his friends.

"The children help tend the gardens." The guide sorted through the herbs, hanging them in small bunches. "Everyone contributes what they can. Age and ability don't matter - only willing hearts."

Selene lifted a loaf of fresh bread, still warm from the morning's baking. The simple abundance surrounding them stood in stark contrast to New Babylon and the GWC's tightly controlled resources. Here, people shared freely without the Mark's tracking system or digital credits.

"The silver coins you carried - you can leave them here if you wish." The guide pointed to a simple wooden box. "Or keep them for those who still require such things outside our walls. We have no need for currency in New Eden."

Asher deposited the coin pouch into the wooden crate. " When in Rome? " he says with a wink to Selene.

Through the winding paths of New Eden, a crowd gathered near the central meeting area. Asher and Selene followed their guide toward the growing circle of people. At its center stood Enoch, his face illuminated with an otherworldly glow as he spoke.

"The streets shimmer with pure gold, transparent as crystal." Enoch's hands moved as he painted pictures with his words. "Each gate is carved from a single pearl, larger than any building in Paradise City or New Babylon."

Children sat cross-legged at his feet, their eyes wide with wonder. Adults leaned forward, hanging on every detail.

"The walls rise higher than mountains, built from jasper and precious stones. No sun or moon lights the city - God's glory fills every corner with living light."

"What about the trees?" A small boy tugged at Enoch's sleeve.

"Ah, the Tree of Life." Enoch knelt beside him. "Its leaves never wither, bearing twelve different fruits. The river of life flows crystal clear from God's throne, nurturing everything it touches."

The crowd moved, and Asher and Selene got a clear view of the stranger. "I'll be honest. The tree of knowledge that Adam and Eve ate from wasn't an apple like people say. It was a chocolate-flavored fruit. That's why they say chocolate is sinful," Enoch joked.

An elderly woman wiped tears from her eyes. "Will there be pain there? Like now?"

"No tears, no death, no sorrow." Enoch touched her shoulder. "I watched Yahshua wipe away every tear. Therefore, He died for each and everyone of us, to restore us as children of Yahweh. He will walk among His people there, not hidden like here. His face shines brighter than any sun."

The crowd murmured, their faces reflecting hope and longing. Some reached out to touch Enoch's garments, as if trying to connect with the heaven he described.

"The music - oh, the music." Enoch closed his eyes, swaying slightly. "Thousands of angels singing in perfect harmony. Their voices shake the very foundations of the city. And when Yahshua joins them..." He paused, overcome with emotion. " The very earth we stand on sings of His glory."

Asher and Selene exchanged glances. The stranger spoke with such vivid detail, such conviction - as if he'd walked those streets himself. The crowd's response unsettled them. These weren't the wild-eyed fanatics Saul had described. These people's faces shone with genuine peace and anticipation.

The small boy tugged at Enoch's sleeve again. "You talk like you lived there. Did you really live with God?"

The crowd fell silent, their attention fixed on Enoch's face. He sat down cross-legged among them, his eyes distant with memory.

"I walked with God for three hundred years in the time before the great flood." Enoch's voice carried across the gathering. "Then He took me to His realm, where I've dwelt these past three millennia."

An older man leaned forward. "You're that Enoch? From Genesis?"

"The seventh from Adam." Enoch nodded. "God showed me His mysteries, taught me the ways of heaven and earth. I watched creation unfold through time beside Him and His Son. A thousand years is but a day in Elysium."

The boy touched Enoch's hand. "But why did you leave heaven to come here?"

"Because darkness spreads across this world again." Enoch drew the child closer. "Like in Noah's time, people have turned from truth to follow their own ways. But God never abandons those who seek Him. He sent me to guide His remnant through these last days."

Whispers rippled through the crowd. Some clutched their Bibles closer, comparing scripture to the man before them.

"In heaven, I learned God's heart." Enoch's eyes met those gathered around him. "His love for each of you burns brighter than all the stars He created. Even now, Yahshua prepares places in that golden city for everyone who stays faithful through these trials."

Asher and Selene lingered at the edge of the crowd, their practiced masks of devotion slipping. This wasn't the radical extremist rhetoric they'd expected to report back to Saul. The stranger spoke of love, of hope - dangerous ideas that could unravel the careful control the GWC maintained.

"He claims to be thousands of years old." Asher whispered to his partner. "Yet looks no older than forty."

Selene watched the children clustering around Enoch, their innocent trust making her stomach twist. "The Mark was supposed to bring unity, peace. But these people..." She gestured at the harmonious community surrounding them.

"They've found it without technology, without control systems." Asher rubbed his unmarked wrist. "Just by following ancient laws and..." He trailed off, unable to rationalize what they witnessed.

The afternoon sun cast long shadows through the canyon as Enoch continued sharing his heavenly memories. His words painted pictures that seemed to hover in the air - streets of gold, crystal seas, living light. The spies leaned forward despite their training, drawn by descriptions that stirred something deep within their hardened hearts.

"What if..." Selene caught herself, shocked by the doubt creeping into her thoughts. Their mission was to infiltrate and destroy this movement, not question the very foundation of their beliefs.

Asher gripped her arm, his fingers trembling slightly. "We need to report back. Saul has to know what's happening here."

But neither spy moved from their spot. The truth in Enoch's words held them frozen, fighting against years of careful conditioning. Their carefully constructed worldview cracked under the weight of simple, powerful truth.

* * *

Asher and Selene approached Enoch after the crowd dispersed. The setting sun painted the canyon walls in deep orange hues.

"Your words moved us deeply." Asher bowed his head. "We'd like to help the cause. What plans does the remnant have?"

Enoch's penetrating gaze studied their faces. "The stadium holds hundreds of believers. Men, women, children - imprisoned for refusing the Mark."

Selene's hand unconsciously touched her unmarked wrist. "The Green World Church claims they're terrorists."

"They're families who chose God's law over man's." Enoch gestured toward the makeshift camp. "Like these people here. The remnant grows daily as more recognize the truth."

"But the stadium's heavily guarded." Asher stepped closer, lowering his voice. "Surely you don't plan to-"

"God opened prison doors for Peter." Enoch's calm certainty made both spies shift uncomfortably. "Tomorrow night, we'll gather outside those walls. The same power that broke chains in Acts still works today."

Selene's training urged her to press for details, but Enoch's next words froze her in place.

"You're welcome to join us. Though Saul might wonder why his trusted agents helped instead of hinder."

The blood drained from their faces. Asher opened his mouth to deny it, but no words came.

"Fear not." Enoch placed a hand on each of their shoulders. "God knows your hearts better than Saul does. You've seen truth today - now go choose what you'll do with it."

The spies departed from Enoch and made their way to the canyon pass. "We have to warn Saul of his plans to attack the" Asher' words trailed off

"Lost?" Enoch's voice cut through the darkness. He stepped out from behind a boulder, his form silhouetted against the starlit sky.

A dark shadow with two incandescent glowing eyes approached them from the north side of the trail. "Rollo stay" Enoch commanded.

Asher reached for his weapon, but Selene grabbed his arm.

"You knew." She lowered her head. "The whole time."

"The Holy Spirit reveals all things." Enoch's eyes held no condemnation. "The maze of canyons ahead is impossible to navigate without the guidance from above. Let me guide you out."

They followed him through twisting passages; the walls pressing closer with each turn. Selene's breath came in sharp gasps as memories flooded back - the day the GWC recruited her to be part of something, but what the GWC offered was false. She could see that now.

"The Mark promised prosperity." Her voice cracked. "Security. A better world."

"And what did it cost?" Enoch stopped at a fork in the path. "Your freedom? Your soul?"

Asher pressed his hand against the canyon wall. "We believed we were serving God through the Green World Church. Creating unity, peace-"

"Through force?" Enoch's words cut deep. "Through persecution of those who choose to follow their Creator's laws instead of man's traditions?"

The wind howled through the canyon like accusing voices. Selene sank to her knees.

"I saw heaven." Enoch knelt beside them. "I walked with God Himself. His kingdom operates on love, not control. On freedom, not force. You stand at a crossroads now - continue serving a system built on lies, or embrace the truth that can set you free."

"Saul will hunt us." Asher helped his wife to her feet. "The GWC never forgets traitors."

"Neither does God forget His children." Enoch gestured toward the path ahead. "Choose now whom you will serve."

Asher and Selene exchanged a long look in the dim starlight. Selene squeezed her husband's hand.

"We choose truth," Asher's voice rang clear through the canyon. "We choose God."

"Please," Selene stepped forward. "We want to be baptized - to start fresh."

Enoch turned to Jose, who had materialized from the shadows. "Brother, prepare the waters for morning. You'll perform their baptism at first light."

Jose's weathered face broke into a smile. "Welcome to the family."

"Now," Enoch's expression grew serious. "Return to Saul. Tell him everything you've witnessed here. And inform him that tomorrow night, every prisoner in that stadium will walk free."

Jose's smile vanished. "What? We can't-"

"Fear not." Enoch raised his hand, silencing Jose's protest. "Just as Moses declared each plague to Pharaoh before it happened, we too will announce God's plans. Let them prepare. Let them fortify their walls. It will make no difference."

"But these are new converts," Jose gestured to the couple. "To send them back-"

"The Lord protects His own." Enoch's eyes held an otherworldly certainty. "Remember the plagues of Egypt. Each one was announced, each one came exactly as promised. Pharaoh's foreknowledge didn't stop God's plan - it proved His power."

Asher straightened his shoulders. "We'll deliver your message."

"The waters will be ready at dawn," Jose conceded, though concern still creased his brow.

The desert morning painted the horizon in soft pinks and golds as Jose led Asher and Selene to the hidden spring. The couple's bare feet pressed into the cool sand while crickets chirped their morning prayers.

"The water's clean here." Jose dipped his hand into the crystalline pool. "Fed by an underground stream."

Asher helped Selene down the rocky path. Her hands trembled as she removed her outer garment, revealing simple clothes beneath.

"I baptize you in the name of the Father, Son, and Holy Spirit." Jose's voice echoed off the canyon walls as he lowered Selene into the water. She emerged gasping, tears mixing with droplets on her face.

Asher followed, his expression peaceful as he rose from the spring. The couple embraced, water streaming from their clothes.

"The old has passed away." Jose handed them dry garments and a pocket Bible. "Behold, the new has come."

Enoch appeared at the spring's edge, his form backlit by the rising sun. "You must deliver the message before nightfall."

"We understand." Asher wrapped an arm around his wife. "Though returning to Saul..."

"Remember, Peter before the Sanhedrin." Enoch's eyes held divine fire. "Let your words be bold. Truth needs no defense - it simply is."

The couple nodded, gathering their courage. They turned toward the city, their wet footprints quickly vanishing into the desert sand.

Jose watched them go, his weathered face creased with worry. "Will they remain faithful under pressure?"

"Their hearts are changed." Enoch placed a hand on Jose's shoulder. "The Holy Spirit goes with them. Now, we prepare for tonight."

***

Saul's office towered above the city, its glass walls reflecting the midday sun. Asher and Selene stood before his desk.

"You found their camp?" Saul's fingers drummed against the polished surface.

"We found truth." Selene's voice rang clearly. "The stranger - Enoch - he walks with divine power. The healings and miracles are real."

Saul's face darkened. "Your mission was to gather intelligence, not fall for parlor tricks."

"We saw heaven's power firsthand." Asher stepped forward. "The Green World Church teaches lies. Your Mark brings death, not salvation."

"Watch your words." Saul rose from his chair. "Remember who gave you everything you have!"

"God gave us everything." Selene touched her pocket Bible hidden inside the chest area of her uniform. "The GWC only offered chains disguised as freedom."

"The stadium prisoners will walk free tonight." Asher met Saul's glare. "Enoch wanted you to know. Like Moses before Pharaoh, he declares God's will."

Saul slammed his fist on the desk. "You dare compare me to-"

"Your Mark burns the flesh." "But God's seal brings healing. The remnant grows because they recognize truth." Selene proclaimed.

"Truth?" Saul barked a laugh. "The GWC united humanity. Ended wars. Created peace."

"Through force and fear." Asher shook his head. "God's kingdom operates on love, not control. We've seen it. We've felt it."

"Guards arrest them, bind their mouths shut," Saul's voice cut like steel. "Take them to the stadium for re-education immediately."

"We serve a higher authority now." Selene straightened her shoulders. "The same God who protected Daniel will protect us."

The guards escorted them out of the office, leaving Saul gripping his desk until his knuckles turned white.

"UnF'n believable," Saul whispered as he paced his office, the setting sun casting long shadows across the polished floor. His reflection fractured across the glass walls - a man whose carefully constructed world showed the first signs of cracking.

He pulled up the holographic display, fingers dancing through ancient texts. "Enoch," he muttered, scrolling past reference after reference. The name appeared in Genesis, mentioned briefly as one who "walked with God."

The words on the screen blurred together: "Enoch walked with God; then he was no more, because God took him." Saul's hand trembled as he accessed the deeper archives. Fragments of ancient manuscripts spoke of a man who witnessed heaven's throne room, who stood in the presence of the Divine.

"Impossible." He collapsed into his chair, rubbing his temples. Yet the evidence mounted - the healings, the prophecies, the uncanny knowledge of scripture. His best agents, trained to resist manipulation, had crumbled before this stranger's words.

The security feed from the stadium showed doubled patrols, reinforced barriers. But Saul's certainty wavered. If this truly was, Enoch returned from walking with God...

He pulled up another file - records of the mysterious cloud that had appeared when the stranger first emerged. The timing aligned perfectly with ancient prophecies about the latter days. The Mark-bearers' unexplained sores, the growing remnant movement, the increasing unrest among the population - all of it pointed to something beyond human understanding.

"Sir." His assistant's voice crackled through the intercom. "The stadium commander requests additional forces for tonight."

Saul stared at the ancient texts, his carefully constructed worldview threatening to unravel. Everything he'd help built through the Green World Church - the unity, the control, the promise of peace - stood challenged by a single figure emerging from the desert.

Saul's fingers hovered over the authorization panel. The stadium's security grid glowed red across his desk display, marking each reinforced position.

"Triple the guard rotation." His voice carried through the command channel. "Shoot to kill any unauthorized personnel within a hundred meters of the perimeter."

The stadium commander's face appeared on the screen. "Sir, we've mounted additional turrets on the east and west walls. Armor-piercing rounds loaded."

"Good." Saul accessed the weapons manifest. "Deploy the experimental sonic deterrents. If they breach the outer gates, activate without warning."

"The prisoners, sir?"

"Acceptable casualties." Saul's jaw clenched. "Better dead than freed by this... imposter."

The manifest updated in real-time as crates of ammunition moved through the security checkpoints. Guards strapped on enhanced body armor, checking weapon sights under the harsh stadium lights.

"Sir," the commander hesitated. "The men are asking - what if the stories are true? What if he really is-" Saul cut him off.

"He's a threat to everything we've built. He is just a terrorist, treat him as such "Nothing more. You have your orders."

The authorization codes flashed green across the screen. Saul pressed his palm against the scanner, feeling the Mark burn slightly as it confirmed his identity. Weapon safeties disengaged across the facility with a series of sharp clicks.

"Maximum force allowed." His words echoed through the command center. "No one approaches those walls. No one leaves. Whatever it takes."

CHAPTER 10

The desert wind whispered across the dunes as Enoch left the hidden sanctuary of New Eden. Stars pierced the velvet sky, their ancient light a reminder of creation's majesty.

"Stay here tonight, Jose. Guard our brothers and sisters. You to Rollo."

Jose nodded, his weathered face etched with concern. "The Lord will protect you."

"And you also, my friend," Enoch replied as he walked off.

Enoch climbed the rocky outcropping overlooking the valley, seeking solitude. The cool night air carried memories of another time, another world - walking with God in Elysium.

He knelt on the stone, closing his eyes. "Father..."

"Your heart troubles you, old friend." Zophiel's voice carried the weight of ages.

Enoch opened his eyes to find the angel seated beside him, wings folded against the starlight. The divine being's form shifted like morning mist, both there and not there.

"The burden grows heavy," Enoch admitted. "So many seek truth, yet the enemy's grip tightens."

"Remember the prophecy." Zophiel's words resonated with celestial authority. "No harm can touch you until the appointed time - one thousand two hundred and sixty days."

"And when does this time begin?"

" Be bold, fear not my friend. It began the day you and Elijah arrived. You and Elijah are the witnesses the Lampstand's sent by Yahweh. You stand on opposite sides of the lamb that speaks like a dragon. Both of you will face the deceiver once he is unmasked." Zophiel looked at the city in the distance. "The false messiah is getting ready to show himself. Your testimony cannot be silenced until you and the other witness confront him directly."

Enoch traced the ancient rod at his side, feeling its power pulse beneath his fingers. "Then there is still work to be done."

"Much work," Zophiel confirmed. "Many must hear truth before darkness falls."

Enoch rose from the stone, his muscles stiff from kneeling. The distant glow of New Babylon's stadium lit the horizon like a false dawn.

"Are you coming with me to the stadium?" The rod hummed against his palm, warm with divine energy.

Zophiel's form shimmered in the starlight. "Wouldn't miss it, but only your eyes will see me until the appointed time, my friend."

The angel's presence shifted like morning fog, nearly invisible yet undeniably there. Enoch sensed rather than saw Zophiel's wings unfold against the night sky.

The path down the rocky slope demanded careful steps. Loose stones clattered beneath Enoch's feet, echoing across the empty desert. The stadium's artificial glare grew stronger with each stride, drowning out the natural beauty of the stars above.

New Babylon's outer walls loomed ahead, their smooth surfaces marked with the Green World Church's symbol - a twisted cross wrapped in thorny vines. Security drones buzzed overhead, their red eyes scanning the darkness.

Enoch pulled his cloak tighter, the desert wind cutting through the worn fabric. The rod pulsed against his side, hidden but ready. Zophiel's invisible presence remained steady, a comfort in the growing shadow of humankind's latest show of roman entertainment.

The stadium entrance approached, its gates wide open for the evening's gathering. Thousands streamed inside, their foreheads and hands Marked with the green sigil of allegiance. Guards stood at attention, weapons ready, scanning each entrant for signs of dissent.

"Remember," Zophiel's voice whispered on the wind, "truth needs no defense - only witnesses."

Enoch strode through the crowd toward the stadium gates. The masses parted before him, their Marked foreheads gleaming under the harsh lights.

"Release those you hold captive." His voice carried across the plaza, silencing the murmur of the crowd. The rod blazed in his right hand.

The guards exchanged glances, their weapons trained on the lone figure. One of them barked out a laugh.

"Move along, old man. Stadium's closed to the unmarked."

"I speak with authority, not of this world." Enoch raised his hand. "Free them."

More guards emerged from their posts, forming a barrier. Their leader stepped forward, green Mark prominent on his forehead. "On your knees, heretic."

The crowd pressed back, creating a circle of space around the confrontation. Whispers rippled through the gathering.

"Saul approaches." The words passed from mouth to mouth until the crowd parted again.

Saul's polished boots clicked against the pavement as he walked toward Enoch. His green robes rustled, adorned with the twisted cross of the Church. A haughty smile played across his features.

"The famous stranger." Saul's voice dripped with false warmth. "Come to join our celebration of unity?"

"I come for those you've imprisoned."

"Imprisoned?" Saul spread his arms wide. "We're protecting them. Teaching them the better way. The only way."

"There is only one Way to life. Your way leads to destruction."

"Bold words from a terrorist." Saul's smile vanished. "The same terrorist who unleashed biological weapons on innocent citizens. Guards-"

"Those Marks you forced upon them brought their own curse." Enoch's words cut through Saul's command. "Release them, or witness Yahweh's power again."

The guards tightened their grips on their weapons. Saul's face darkened with rage, but uncertainty flickered in his eyes.

Saul's jaw clenched. He jabbed a finger at Enoch. "Take him."

Six guards broke formation, their boots pounding against the pavement as they rushed forward. The crowd pressed back further, creating a wider circle around the confrontation. The guards' weapons gleamed under the harsh stadium lights.

The first guard reached for Enoch's arm. A pulse of invisible force erupted from where Enoch stood. The guards flew backward as if struck by a tidal wave, their bodies tumbling through the air. They crashed into the crowd twenty feet away, scattering people like bowling pins.

Screams erupted. The remaining guards stumbled back, their weapons trembling in their hands. Saul's face drained of color.

More guards poured from the stadium entrance, forming a defensive line. Their boots scraped against concrete as they shuffled backward, maintaining a distance from the stranger who stood unmoved.

"What sorcery is this?" Saul's voice cracked. His hand clutched at the twisted cross hanging from his neck.

The fallen guards groaned, struggling to rise. Their uniforms were torn, faces scratched from their impact with the ground. None dared approach again.

Enoch remained still, his cloak barely stirring in the evening breeze. The rod hummed against his side, its power flowing through him like a river of light.

The crowd pushed further back, their earlier confidence shattered. Some fled toward the city gates, while others pressed against the stadium walls, unwilling to turn their backs on the scene unfolding before them.

Enoch raised the rod, its ancient wood gleaming with an inner light cast long shadows across the plaza. The crowd gasped as the rod's glow intensified, bathing the scene of divine radiance.

"This is your final warning." His voice carried across the stunned silence. "Release God's people or face His judgment."

Saul's face contorted with rage and fear. "You dare threaten-"

Thunder cracked overhead. The clear night sky swirled with sudden clouds, their depths illuminated by flashes of lightning. Wind whipped through the plaza, scattering debris and forcing people to shield their faces.

"Your prisons cannot hold what God has freed." Enoch struck the ground with his rod.

The earth trembled. Deep rumbles echoed from beneath the stadium's foundations. Cracks spider-webbed across the concrete, spreading outward from where the rod had touched.

The stadium's walls groaned. Metal screamed. A section of the outer wall collapsed inward, revealing the cells hidden within. Hundreds of unmarked prisoners stared out through the breach, their chains falling away as if made of smoke.

"The Lord breaks the chains of the oppressed." Enoch's words cut through the chaos. "Come forth!"

The prisoners streamed through the gap, blinking in the rod's holy light. Guards scrambled to stop them but found themselves rooted to the spot, unable to move.

Saul staggered backward, his polished facade crumbling. "Stop them! Someone stop-"

Another thunderclap drowned out his words. Lightning struck the stadium's highest point, shattering the Green World Church's twisted cross. The broken pieces rained down, forcing Saul to dive for cover.

The freed prisoners gathered behind Enoch, their faces transformed by joy and wonder. Some wept, others embraced, all moved by the power of their deliverance.

Through the chaos of the crumbling stadium walls, Enoch spotted Asher and Selene at the edge of the crowd. The couple's faces reflected the divine light from his rod, their expressions a mix of awe and uncertainty.

"Asher," Enoch called out. The man's head snapped up, his wife clutching his arm. "Take these freed souls to New Eden."

Asher stepped forward, his weathered face lined with concern. "But the patrols-"

"The Lord's cloud will shield your path." Enoch raised the rod, and a familiar mist formed around the gathered prisoners. "Guide them through the desert as Moses led our ancestors."

Selene released her husband's arm and moved among the freed captives, her gentle voice organizing them into groups. "Come, brothers and sisters. Freedom awaits in the wilderness."

"What of you?" Asher asked, watching as his wife directed the first group toward the city gates.

"My work here isn't finished." Enoch's gaze turned back to the stadium, where guards still stood frozen and Saul cowered behind a fallen piece of masonry. "The Lord has more to show this place."

The mist thickened around Asher and the prisoners, obscuring them from the watching crowd. Their footsteps faded into the night, leaving Enoch alone before the broken stadium.

Zophiel's invisible presence brushed against his consciousness. "They will reach New Eden safely."

Enoch gripped the rod tighter, its power thrumming through his bones. The night was far from over.

Enoch turned to face the remaining crowd, his rod casting divine light across their Marked faces. The stadium's ruins smoldered behind him, concrete dust settling in the night air.

"Choose now between the Creator of Heaven and Earth or this false church. Your eternal fate hangs in this moment."

The crowd shifted, hundreds of eyes reflecting the rod's glow. Guards lowered their weapons, the freeze holding them having lifted. Saul emerged from behind the fallen masonry, his green robes stained with dust.

Silence stretched across the plaza. No one stepped forward. No voice spoke up for the truth. The Marks on their foreheads seemed to pulse with an unholy light.

Enoch's shoulders dropped. He turned his back on the crowd, his cloak sweeping across the cracked pavement.

"Fire, shoot the terrorist," Saul shouted

The sky split open. Flames poured down like rain, white-hot columns of divine fire that engulfed the stadium and its surroundings. The crowd's screams cut short as the inferno consumed them. Metal melted. Stone cracked. The remaining walls collapsed in a thunderous roar.

When the flames receded, only ash remained. Saul lay face-down at the edge of the destruction, his green robes scorched but his body untouched. He pushed himself to his knees, staring at the smoking ruin where his followers and all his GWC Guards had stood moments before.

The rod's light dimmed, casting long shadows across the devastation. And not a single righteous soul could be found among them. No one had chosen truth over comfort, Yahweh over the Green World Church.

* * *

At the GWC HQ, Las Vegas, their busying council chamber. Helena Vale's face turned white and reflected on the polished obsidian table. The holographic display revealed a smoking crater where the stadium used to be. The thermal readings were still extremely high.

"Impossible." She jabbed a finger at the feed. "Our systems detected no energy signatures, no radiation, no chemical agents. Nothing."

The council members shifted anxiously in their seats, their green robes rustling. Emergency lights pulsed across their faces, casting sickly shadows.

"Look at the pattern." Councilor Waters zoomed the image. "Perfect circles of destruction, but Saul..." He enhanced the footage of their head priest, stumbling through the ash. "Completely unharmed."

"Get me, Saul. Now." Helena's voice cut through the murmurs. "I want him on the first transport to Las Vegas."

"Already dispatched, Madam Leader." Her aide tapped rapidly on a tablet. "ETA forty minutes."

"And what of our containment protocols?" She turned to the military liaison. "How does one man bypass every security measure we've implemented?"

General Morris cleared his throat. "With respect, Madam Leader, we're not dealing with technology. The energy readings match nothing in our database. It's as if-"

"Don't." Helena slammed her palm on the table. "I won't entertain supernatural explanations. There's a logical scientific answer. Find it."

With a flicker, the screen revealed new angles of the destruction. Ash, forming perfect circles. The melted steel. The untouched ground where Saul had fallen.

"Someone get me answers before Saul arrives." Helena's Mark pulsed against her forearm. "I want to know what we're dealing with. And how to stop it."

The council chamber erupted into activity, screens lighting up as analysts pored over the footage. But no one could explain how a single man with a wooden staff had reduced their most secure facility to ash.

CHAPTER II

The desert wind whipped around Enoch as Zophiel set him down on the rocky outcrop. Below, Las Vegas's neon sprawl pierced the night like a wound in the darkness. In the distance, smoke still rose from New Babylon, a grim reminder of what had transpired.

Enoch sank to his knees, the rough stone biting through his clothes. His shoulders shook as he pressed his palms against the cold ground.

"Three hundred souls." His voice cracked. "Not one turned to Yahweh. Not one."

Zophiel's form shimmered, more starlight than substance. "You gave them a choice, Enoch. As He gave a choice to Adam in the garden."

"I saw their faces." Enoch's fingers dug into the dirt. "The moment before... they could have chosen life. They could have-" He choked on the words.

"Like Lot in Sodom." Zophiel's voice carried the weight of millennia. "Some hearts harden beyond reaching. Even when angels walk among them."

The wind carried the acrid smell of smoke, mixing with the artificial sweetness of the city below. Enoch pushed himself to his feet, his staff scraping against the stone.

"I failed them." Blood dripped from his clenched fist. "Just as Sodom failed. Just as Gomorrah-"

"You showed them truth." Zophiel's light pulsed brighter. "Their choice was their own. As it was in the days of Noah, so it shall be."

Enoch stared at the city lights, each one representing countless souls still trapped in darkness. The Mark of the GWC glowed from buildings and billboards, a false beacon leading humanity astray.

"How many more?" Enoch's whisper barely carried over the wind. "How many more will choose death over His love?"

Zophiel's presence enveloped him like a cloak of stars. "That is not for us to know. Only to witness."

The lights of Las Vegas grew closer as Enoch descended the mountain path, his staff tapping against loose rocks. The GWC headquarters loomed ahead - a gleaming tower of glass and steel that pierced the sky like a modern Tower of Babel.

"Their hearts are hardened, but not beyond His reach," Zophiel's voice carried on the wind. "Remember Nineveh."

Enoch strode through the grand plaza toward the building's entrance. Security guards reached for their weapons but froze as his presence washed over them. The lobby fell silent as he entered, his dusty robes a stark contrast to the polished marble and sleek technology.

"Hear the words of the Living God!" His voice filled the space, carrying to every floor through the open atrium. "For He desires not the death of sinners, but that all should turn to Him and live!"

People gathered at the railings above, drawn by the power in his words. The Mark of the GWC pulsed an angry red on their foreheads.

"You bear the Mark of bondage, but He offers the seal of freedom!" Enoch raised his staff. "As Jonah proclaimed to Nineveh - yet forty days, and your systems shall fall. But if you turn from this evil, if you cast off these chains of darkness, His mercy awaits!"

A security team burst from the elevators, weapons raised.

"The same God who delivered Daniel from the lion's den stands ready to deliver you!" Enoch's words thundered through the building. "Choose this day whom you will serve! If the Lord be God, follow Him. But if Baal be god, then follow him."

The security team leader stepped forward, hand trembling on his weapon. "Sir, you need to leave-"

"'Come out of her, my people,'" Enoch quoted, his voice gentle now but carrying no less power. "'That ye be not partakers of her sins, and that ye receive not of her plagues.' The choice stands before you - life or death, blessing or curse. Choose life that both you and your children may live."

Enoch strode into the courtyard, his staff striking the marble with each step. The afternoon sun caught the golden GWC emblems adorning the walls, their artificial gleam a mockery of divine light. News cameras swiveled to track his movement, broadcasting his presence across the globe.

"Fear God and give Him glory!" His voice carried across the plaza, drawing people to windows and balconies. "For the hour of His judgment has come. Worship Him who made heaven and earth, the sea and springs of water!"

A crowd gathered, phones raised to capture his words. Security personnel formed a perimeter but kept their distance, uncertainty evident in their stance.

"Babylon is fallen!" Enoch raised his staff toward the towering headquarters. "That great city which made all nations drink of the wine of the wrath of her fornication."

Inside the building's executive floor, GWC leaders crowded around monitors displaying his broadcast. Their Marks pulsed an angry red as his words penetrated their carefully constructed facade.

"If anyone worships the beast and his image, and receives his Mark on their forehead or hand, they themselves shall drink of the wine of the wrath of God!"

The crowd's murmuring grew louder. Some clutched their Marked foreheads, while others fell to their knees.

"Here is the patience of the saints!" Enoch's voice thundered across the courtyard. "Here are those who keep the commandments of God and the faith of Yahshua!"

The GWC's emergency broadcast system blared to life, but Enoch's words cut through the noise:

"Remember the Sabbath day, to keep it holy! Six days you shall labor and do all your work, but the seventh day is the Sabbath of the Lord your God!"

A woman in pristine white robes pushed through the crowd, her GWC Mark gleaming gold instead of the usual red. Her heels clicked against the marble as she approached Enoch.

"I am Helena, High Priestess of the Global World Church." Her voice carried across the courtyard through hidden speakers. "Your blasphemy ends here."

She held up an ancient scroll, its edges gilded in gold. "The Grand Pope sanctified these laws himself in the year five hundred and thirty-eight. For fifteen hundred years, the faithful have followed our traditions. Who are you to question centuries of divine guidance?"

"Traditions of men." Enoch's staff struck the ground. "You teach false doctrines the commandments of men, making void the word of God."

"Every nation follows our laws." Helena's eyes narrowed. "Every tongue and tribe acknowledges our authority. The Mark we bear is proof of God's and Mother-Earth blessing."

"Did not Jezebel claim the same? Did not all Israel bow to Baal save seven thousand?"

"Our lineage traces back to Peter himself,"

"Thus says the Lord," Enoch cut through her words. "'This people draws near to Me with their mouth, and honors Me with their lips, but their heart is far from Me.'"

Helena's face flushed. "The Grand Pope changed the law by divine right-"

"He shall speak pompous words against the Most High, shall persecute the saints of the Most High, and shall intend to change times and law." Enoch's voice carried the weight of prophecy. "Daniel spoke of this very moment. You claim authority to change His eternal law, yet it is written: 'I am the Lord, I do not change.'"

"Millions follow our ways-"

"Enter by the narrow gate," Enoch replied. "For wide is the gate and broad is the way that leads to destruction, and there are many who go in by it."

The crowd shifted uneasily, their eyes darting between Helena and Enoch. The Mark on their foreheads pulsed in sync with the massive GWC displays that towered above the plaza.

A young security guard stepped forward, his hand trembling as he reached for the Mark on his forehead. Blood trickled down his face as he clawed at it.

"I-I remember." His voice cracked. "My grandmother. She used to read from an old Bible. Before they burned them all."

Helena whirled toward him. "Officer Martinez, remember your oath."

"She told me about the Sabbath." Martinez pulled off his GWC badge and let it clatter to the ground. "How they changed it. How they-" He fell to his knees before Enoch. "Please, help me remove this, Mark."

"Traitor!" Helena's voice boomed through the plaza speakers. "The Mark is permanent. The choice was made."

"Nothing is permanent in the face of God's mercy," Enoch said. He placed his hand on Martinez's forehead. "Your faith has made you whole."

The Mark faded from Martinez's skin like mist in sunlight. He touched his forehead, tears streaming down his face.

Others in the crowd stirred. A woman in business attire stepped forward. Then a janitor. A delivery driver. Each one choosing, each one facing Helena's fury as they turned away from the system that had bound them.

"You will lose everything!" Helena's voice shook with rage. "Your homes, your wealth, your status-"

"For what profit is it to a man if he gains the whole world and loses his own soul?" Enoch's words cut through her threats.

The choice hung in the air like a physical thing. Some turned away, clutching their Marks and hurrying back to the safety of the GWC tower. Others stepped forward, ready to face whatever came next.

Enoch raised his staff toward the heavens, its weathered wood gleaming with an inner light. The crowd fell silent, even the wind seeming to hold its breath.

"For the Lord knows your hearts." his voice rolled like thunder across the plaza. "Those who turn to Yahweh and His commandments, your Marks shall vanish. A clean heart will be made new within you."

His gaze swept across the assembled masses, landing finally on Helena. "But for those who choose the Global World Church and man's counterfeit laws, I pronounce the first plague upon you - loathsome sores shall afflict your flesh."

The staff struck the marble with a crack that echoed off the glass towers. Helena's scream pierced the air as angry red welts erupted across her exposed skin. She clawed at her face, her golden Mark now surrounded by festering sores.

The plague spread through the crowd like wildfire. Those who still bore the GWC Mark collapsed in agony as boils covered their bodies. The pristine plaza descended into chaos as the Marked stumbled and fell, their cries echoing off the buildings.

"My face!" Helena writhed on the ground, her white robes now stained with blood from her wounds. "Make it stop!"

But those who had chosen to follow God's law stood untouched, their skin clear, their Marks dissolved away. Martinez helped others to their feet as they emerged from the plague unscathed, their faces reflecting both wonder and horror at the scene unfolding around them.

The sores spread across the city, then beyond. Reports flooded in from Seattle, Portland, Los Angeles - everywhere the GWC held sway along the West Coast, the Marked fell victim to the plague.

Enoch turned to Martinez, who stood amid the chaos of screaming GWC followers clutching their sore-covered faces. "Take these freed souls to safety. A pillar will guide you through the desert. - follow it without question."

Martinez nodded, his clear forehead glistening with sweat. He raised his voice above the din. "Everyone who's been cleansed, gather here!"

A group of about fifty people huddled together - office workers, security guards, maintenance staff - all Marked no more. They cast nervous glances at their former colleagues writhing on the ground.

The air shimmered and Zophiel materialized, starlight coalescing into an almost-human form. "I will show you the way. The remnant awaits in the wilderness."

Damien Folk burst through the GWC building's doors, flanked by a squad of security forces in tactical gear. Despite the plague affecting his Marked soldiers, they raised their weapons.

"Arrest that man!" Folk's face contorted with rage beneath his festering sores. "He's responsible for this attack!"

"Go now," Enoch commanded Martinez's group. "Follow the angel's light."

As Zophiel led the freed people toward the city's edge, security forces surrounded Enoch. He made no move to resist as they cuffed his hands behind his back.

"Your plagues and parlor tricks won't save you now," Folk spat, wiping blood from a burst boil. "Take him to containment."

The guards marched Enoch into the GWC tower's depths, their Marked faces twisted in pain with each step. His staff clattered to the ground, abandoned in the plaza where moments before he had pronounced God's judgment.

Behind them, a pillar of light rose into the darkening sky, guiding Martinez and the freed souls toward sanctuary in the desert.

CHAPTER 12

The cell block's fluorescent lights cast harsh shadows across Enoch's face as he sat cross-legged on the concrete floor. His wrists bore raw marks from the restraints, but his expression remained peaceful.

"You speak of freedom," a burly guard named Thompson leaned against the bars, scratching at the sores that covered his neck. "But look where that got you."

"These walls cannot contain the truth." Enoch's gaze met the guard's. "Just as those Marks cannot contain your soul."

Two inmates in the adjacent cell pressed closer to listen. One of them, a former tech executive named Ronald, was arrested for refusing the new digital currency system and the GWC Mark.

"My wife and kids," Ronald's voice cracked. "They're still out there, still Marked. I couldn't protect them."

"The Lord is their shepherd," Enoch replied. "His rod and staff will comfort them, just as He guides those who seek Him now."

Thompson's one of the GWC guards' radio crackled with reports of more riots breaking out across the city. The plague of sores had overwhelmed emergency services.

"The system is breaking down," Thompson muttered, wincing as he shifted his weight. "Nothing's working like they promised."

"Because it was built on lies," Enoch stood, approaching the bars. "But God's truth stands eternal. His law was written not on silicon chips, but on tablets of stone."

A female guard named Rodriguez appeared with the evening meal cart. She paused, listening as Enoch spoke of God's mercy and justice. The food grew cold as more guards and inmates gathered.

"I was there when He formed the mountains," Enoch's words filled the corridor. "When He set the boundaries of the seas. His power dwells not in digital networks or artificial systems, but in the hearts of those who choose Him."

One by one, guards and prisoners alike sank to their knees. Thompson removed his cap, revealing the Mark on his forehead now surrounded by angry welts.

"How do we choose?" he whispered.

"Reject the Mark of man," Enoch touched the bars separating them. "Accept God's law written on your heart. The sores that plague you will vanish, and you will be made clean."

Rodriguez unclipped her keys with trembling hands. "Show us."

Thompson's keys rattled against the lock. The cell door swung open with a metallic groan. Enoch stepped out, his bare feet silent on the cold concrete floor. Guards and inmates formed a circle around him, their faces etched with pain and desperation.

"The Mark enslaved us." Rodriguez pressed her hand against the welts on her neck. "We believed their promises of prosperity."

"God offers freedom through His grace." Enoch raised his hands. "Kneel with me."

They sank to their knees, the guards' uniforms mixing with inmate jumpsuits in a circle of shared humanity. Ronald wiped tears from his face.

"Repeat after me," Enoch bowed his head. "Heavenly Father, I come before you as a sinner."

Their voices merged in rough whispers, echoing off the prison walls.

"I acknowledge my transgressions against Your holy law. I accept Your Son's sacrifice for my sins."

Thompson removed his cap, revealing the Mark that had brought such suffering. His voice cracked as he spoke the words.

"Write Your law upon my heart. Cleanse me of all unrighteousness. I reject the Mark of man and choose Your eternal truth."

As their prayers filled the cell block, the angry welts began to fade from their skin. Rodriguez gasped, touching her now-smooth neck. Others followed suit, discovering their sores had vanished.

"The Lord has heard your prayers," Enoch smiled. "His Spirit now dwells within you."

Thompson stood, his face transformed by joy. "We must share this with others."

"Yes," Enoch nodded. "But remember - the path ahead requires courage. The world will oppose those who choose God's truth."

The new believers gathered closer, their faces glowing with renewed purpose. The harsh prison lighting seemed softer now, as if touched by divine grace.

For three days and nights, Enoch's voice carried through the prison corridors. The concrete walls amplified his message as shifts of guards rotated through, each bringing fresh faces hungry for truth.

"The Mark promised prosperity," a night guard named Peters removed his cap, revealing fresh sores. "But it brought only pain."

The growing congregation gathered in the common area, their prison uniforms and guard outfits no longer symbols of division. Thompson organized the meetings, ensuring they remained undetected by prison authorities.

"We must be careful," Rodriguez passed out contraband Bibles she'd smuggled from the evidence room. "The GWC has eyes everywhere."

Through barred windows, they watched surveillance drones patrol the perimeter. The prison's AI system logged every movement, every conversation. But Ronalds had worked in tech - he knew how to loop the security feeds.

"My wife sent word," Ronald whispered during the evening gathering. "The GWC is implementing mandatory weekly scans. They're hunting for those who've rejected the Mark."

The group huddled closer as Enoch spoke of persecution in ancient times, of believers who'd faced similar trials. Their numbers swelled with each shift change - kitchen staff, maintenance workers, even administrative personnel slipped into their meetings.

"They control the food supply," Thompson reported on the third day. "No Mark, no rations. They're tightening the noose."

But faith grew stronger than fear. The converted guards smuggled food to those who'd chosen God's law over the GWC's Mark. Rodriguez coordinated with sympathetic staff in other prison blocks, spreading Enoch's message through whispered conversations and handwritten notes.

"The Spirit moves among us," Enoch touched the bars of his cell, now a pulpit rather than a prison. "But remember - our battle is not against flesh and blood, but against the powers of darkness."

The sound of boots echoed through the corridor. A squad of GWC enforcement officers approached, their weapons charged. The new believers scattered to their positions, their faces calm despite the danger. They'd chosen their path, knowing the cost of their conviction.

* * *

In the sterile confines of the GWC's research facility, Dr. Sarah Chen adjusted her protective goggles and placed Enoch's staff on the examination table. Under the harsh laboratory lights, Dr. Chen saw the staff was made of ancient olive wood.

"Initial scan shows a cellular structure of just plain old wood." She passed a handheld device over its length. The readings flickered erratically across her screen.

Dr. David Weber positioned the portable x-ray unit. "The density readings show this to be just old olive wood. How can such power come from just a piece of wood?"

The staff lay motionless as they subjected it to test after test. Spectrometers whirred. Mass analyzers hummed. Each device returned impossible results or simply malfunctioned when brought near the artifact.

"Look at this." Weber pointed to the x-ray display. Where the staff should have cast a shadow, there was only a brilliant white void. "It's as if the radiation passes straight through, yet our physical tests show it's completely solid."

Chen ran her fingers along the surface. "No tool Marks, no grain pattern. The molecular structure defies classification."

"Try the electron microscope."

Under maximum magnification, the staff's surface revealed no conventional atomic structure. Instead, swirling patterns of light danced across the monitor, forming and reforming in endless combinations.

"This isn't wood." Chen stepped back from the microscope. "It's not metal, or any known composite. By all scientific standards, this object shouldn't exist. How is it possible for some equipment to show olive wood and others to show these results?"

Weber started a spectral analysis. The machine sparked and shut down. "Third equipment failure today. Whatever this thing is, our technology can't process it."

The staff remained unchanged by their attempts to understand it, its surface cool to the touch despite the battery of energy-based tests they'd subjected it to. The scientists' notes filled with questions rather than answers, their instruments unable to penetrate its mysteries.

Dr. Chen secured the staff in the industrial vice while Weber calibrated the diamond-tipped saw. The blade's teeth gleamed under the fluorescent lights.

"Recording test 47-B, attempting cross-sectional analysis." Weber adjusted his safety goggles. "Initiating cut at precisely 0900 hours."

The saw whirred to life. As the blade descended toward the ancient wood, the air crackled with static electricity. The overhead lights flickered.

"Wait-" Chen stepped back. "Something's wrong."

A blast of pure white light erupted in the center of the lab. The scientists shielded their eyes as the brilliance intensified, but it pierced through their closed eyelids, searing into their retinas.

The figure of Zophiel materialized within the radiance. The angel's form shifted between human and otherworldly, impossible to focus on directly. With fluid grace, Zophiel reached for the staff.

"Such arrogance." The angel's voice resonated through their bones. "To think mortal instruments could dissect divine providence."

The staff lifted from the vice, floating into Zophiel's grasp. The scientists collapsed to their knees, clutching their faces as the light burned deeper.

"Your eyes sought to pierce holy mysteries. Now they shall see only darkness."

Chen screamed as her vision dissolved into blackness. Weber clawed at his eyes, but could no longer perceive even shadows. The light vanished, taking Zophiel and the staff with it. Only darkness remained for the scientists who had dared to cut into God's instrument.

Emergency alarms blared through the facility. Security personnel rushed in to find the two scientists sprawled on the floor, their eyes wide open but unseeing, the staff nowhere to be found.

* * *

In the depths of the GWC detention center, Enoch sat cross-legged on the cold concrete floor of his cell. The fluorescent lights buzzed overhead, casting harsh shadows across the stark walls.

A guard passed by, scratching at the festering sores that covered his arms. The first plague had spread through the facility like wildfire, affecting everyone who bears the Mark of the GWC.

The air shifted. A noticeable temperature drop flowed through the cell. The fluorescent lights above flickered and died, plunging the corridor into darkness. A soft, white glow emanated from the corner of Enoch's cell.

Zophiel materialized, the angel's form both there and not there, handing the ancient staff to Enoch. "Your work here is done. Let's not lose this again."

The cell door dissolved into light. Alarms blared through the facility as Enoch stepped into the corridor. Guards rushed toward them, but froze mid-stride as Zophiel raised a hand. Time itself seemed to pause.

Three floors above, in the medical wing, Helena Vale paced the sterile laboratory. Her arms were covered in weeping sores that no amount of experimental treatment could cure.

"We've isolated the compound." The lead researcher held up a vial of iridescent liquid. "Early tests show complete remission of symptoms within hours."

Helena reached for the vial with trembling hands. Her legs buckled beneath her. She collapsed onto the white tile floor, her breath coming in ragged gasps.

"Get medical support in here now!" The researcher dropped to his knees beside her.

But Helena's eyes had already glazed over, her skin mottled with the dark patches of advanced infection. The cure she'd fought so desperately to create lay just inches from her outstretched fingers.

At the detention level, Enoch and Zophiel walked untouched through the frozen tableau of guards and alarms. The staff hummed with quiet power in Enoch's grip as they passed through the outer walls of the facility and into the night beyond.

CHAPTER 13

In the GWC's west coast headquarters, Damien Folk stood at the floor-to-ceiling windows of what had been Helena's office. The city sprawled below, its streets emptier than usual as more citizens succumbed to the plague.

The door opened behind him. His new assistant placed a tablet on the glass desk. "The vote was unanimous, sir. The council has appointed you as president of the West Coast Division."

Damien's reflection stared back at him in the window. Dark circles ringed his eyes from sleepless nights. The sores had spread across his neck despite the experimental treatments.

The tablet chimed. Messages flooded the screen - reports from GWC chapters across the region. His fingers traced across the surface, opening each one.

"Seattle branch reports thirty percent of Marked followers hospitalized."

"Portland leadership quarantined."

"San Francisco temple closed because of staff infections."

"Los Angeles congregation down sixty percent."

The messages blurred together. Names of the dead. Statistics of the infected. Facilities shuttered. Congregations scattered.

"Sir?" His assistant cleared his throat. "There's a priority message from Central."

Damien tapped the flashing icon. The holographic display flickered to life, projecting the gaunt face of the GWC's Supreme Council Chairman.

"The situation is dire, Folk. We've lost contact with our European branches. The Asian divisions report mass defections. Africa has gone dark." The Chairman's hand shook as he wiped sweat from his brow. "This plague... it's not natural. Our best minds can't explain why it only affects those who've taken the Mark."

"What are your orders?"

"Find this Enoch. Whatever it takes. He started this, and he must know how to end it." The Chairman's image flickered. "The future of our church depends on it."

The transmission cut out, leaving Damien alone with the endless stream of reports. He pressed his palm against the cool glass, watching the sun set behind the mountains. Helena's death had thrust him into power at the worst possible moment. The GWC was crumbling, and he had to hold it together.

Damien slammed his fist on the desk, scattering tablets across its surface. "The Commandment Keepers murdered Helena. They're working with this Enoch character."

The emergency council chamber buzzed with murmurs from the assembled GWC leaders. Screens displayed footage of Helena's last moments - her body covered in weeping sores, her breath coming in ragged gasps.

"Our intelligence confirms increased activity at known CK gathering spots," A security chief pointed to a map dotted with red Markers. "Underground meetings, secret baptisms, stockpiling supplies."

"They've been spreading lies about our Mark." Another council member touched the green symbol on his wrist. "Claiming it's some kind of divine judgment."

"These extremists must be stopped." Damien paced the length of the chamber. "Helena built this division from nothing. She united the faiths under one banner. And now these... these fanatics dare to strike at us?"

A younger council member raised her hand. "Sir, our medical teams report something strange. The sores only appear on those who've received our Mark. The CK members show no symptoms."

"Of course not. They developed some kind of targeted bioweapon." Damien's voice cracked. "Helena was their first target. A message to us all."

The council chamber's screens flickered, displaying scenes of chaos from GWC temples across the region. Marked followers writhed in agony while the unmarked stood untouched.

"Issue an order." Damien's eyes burned with fury. "Every known Commandment Keeper is to be shot. Every suspected sympathizer arrested and questioned. We'll root out this infection at its source."

But deep in his gut, a small voice whispered doubts he couldn't silence. Why had their Mark, meant to unite humanity under one faith, become a source of such suffering? Why did the unmarked remain healthy while the faithful endured such torment?

He pushed the thoughts away. There was no room for doubt. Helena's death demanded vengeance, and he would deliver it.

Damien Folk drummed his fingers on the polished surface of his desk. "Somebody bring Saul to me here at once."

Two guards rushed from the office. Minutes stretched like hours until heavy footsteps echoed down the corridor. Saul strode in, his black uniform pristine despite the chaos engulfing the city.

"You wanted to see me, sir?" Saul's boots clicked as he came to attention.

"The time for half measures is over." Damien rose from his chair. "These Commandment Keepers mock us with their immunity while our people suffer. Helena's death will not go unanswered."

"What are your orders?"

"Kill anyone found without the Mark." Damien's voice dropped to a whisper. "No arrests. No questions. No mercy."

Saul's eyes widened for a fraction of a second before his face hardened into a mask. "The entire city?"

"The entire west coast." Damien turned to face the window. "I want search teams going door to door. Anyone refusing the Mark dies on the spot. Make examples of them. Let their bodies serve as warnings."

"Some of them have children—"

"Did they show mercy to Helena?" Damien spun around. "Did they spare her as the sores ate away at her flesh? Execute the order, Saul. Now."

Saul snapped to attention, his jaw clenched. "Yes, sir. It will be done."

"One more thing." Damien picked up Helena's tablet, her final report still displayed on the screen. "Find me this Enoch. Bring him to me alive. I want him to witness what his rebellion has wrought before he dies."

Saul's boots echoed through the marble halls of GWC headquarters. "First things first, we have to clear our own house." His hand rested on the holster at his hip. "Those prison converts pose the greatest threat - they know our security protocols."

Two squads of armed guards fell in behind him as he strode toward the security center. The night shift supervisor jumped to attention as they entered.

"Pull up the personnel files for Central Detention." Saul leaned over the supervisor's shoulder as names and faces flashed across the screens. "Cross-reference with shift schedules from the past few days - anyone who had contact with the prisoner called Enoch."

Red flags appeared next to dozens of names. Guards who'd requested transfers after Enoch's escape. Inmates whose behavior had dramatically changed. Staff who'd stopped attending mandatory GWC services.

"There." Saul jabbed his finger at the screen. "Start with the guard barracks. Team One, take the east wing. Team Two, west wing. Shoot on sight - we can't risk them spreading more dissent."

The guards moved with practiced efficiency through the compound. Gunshots echoed through the corridors. Screams cut short. Bodies of former colleagues slumped in doorways and hallways.

In the prison blocks, inmates who'd converted under Enoch's teaching pressed against their cell bars, singing hymns as the execution squads approached. They didn't run or beg. They faced their killers with peaceful expressions, dying with prayers on their lips.

Saul watched the security feeds, Marking off names as each target fell. "Send cleanup crews to dispose of the bodies. I want no martyrs for the resistance to rally around."

The night shift supervisor's hands trembled as he typed commands. "Sir, some of these people - I've known them for years."

"They're traitors now." Saul's voice was ice. "Corrupted by that false prophet. The only mercy we can show is a quick death."

The condemned walked in silence, their bare feet leaving tracks in the morning dew that coated the courtyard's grass. GWC guards herded them into neat rows, rifle barrels pressed against backs and shoulders.

Saul paced before them, his boots clicking against the concrete. Camera drones hovered overhead, broadcasting the scene across the city. The rising sun cast long shadows across faces Marked by peaceful acceptance.

"You stand accused of betraying the Mother Church." Saul's voice carried across the courtyard. "Of spreading lies and discord among the faithful. Of following the terrorist Enoch and his blasphemous teachings."

A woman in the front row lifted her chin. "We follow only truth."

"Silence!" Saul backhanded her. Blood trickled from her split lip, but her expression remained serene.

The massive screens on the GWC headquarters' facade flickered to life. Damien Folk's face loomed over the courtyard, his eyes hard as stone.

"Let this serve as a message to all who would reject unity." Damien's amplified voice echoed off the buildings. "By my authority as President of the West Coast Division, I declare that any member of the Commandment Keepers, any follower of the terrorist Enoch, anyone found without the Mark of the GWC will be executed without trial."

The condemned began to sing, their voices rising in harmony. The guards shifted uncomfortably as the hymn filled the air.

"Ready!" Saul raised his hand. The guards lifted their rifles.

The singing grew louder.

"Aim!"

The morning sun caught the tears streaming down the faces of the condemned, but their voices never wavered.

"Fire!"

The courtyard erupted in gunfire. Bodies crumpled to the grass. The singing stopped.

* * *

Jose's fingers trembled as he adjusted the dials on the shortwave radio. The massacre footage played on repeat across every channel - bodies sprawled on blood-stained grass, GWC guards standing over them with smoking rifles. His stomach churned at the sight of former friends and colleagues gunned down in cold blood.

The radio crackled with static as he found the right frequency. He'd modified this unit himself, routing it through a maze of defunct satellites to avoid GWC detection. The signal would bounce between remote locations, impossible to trace back to its source.

He pressed the transmit button. "Brothers and sisters." His voice caught. He cleared his throat and started again. "Brothers and sisters, you've seen what happened at GWC headquarters. But do not let your hearts be troubled."

The faces of the condemned flashed through his mind - their peaceful expressions even as rifles pressed against their backs. Their voices raised in song until the very end.

"To all who are heavy laden, remember the Lord's yoke is light." Jose leaned closer to the microphone, speaking barely above a whisper. "Those who fear the Lord, fear not what man can do. The mountains of hope await. Find your way to the wilderness."

He repeated the message three times in different languages, using the code phrases they'd established. The faithful would understand - head for the remote peaks where Enoch's followers had established sanctuary. GWC surveillance couldn't reach the deep canyons or hidden caves. They were unpassable.

Jose switched off the radio and began dismantling it piece by piece. He'd dispose of the components in different locations across the city. The GWC would be monitoring all communications now, hunting for any sign of organized resistance.

The warrant for Enoch's arrest blazed across every screen in sight as he stepped out of the hidden broadcast room. His friend's face stared down from buildings and billboards, labeled as the most dangerous terrorist in history. A billion-credit bounty for information leading to his capture.

* * *

Enoch knelt in the desert cave, his head bowed under the weight of the news. The massacre victims' faces burned in his mind - men, women, and children who'd chosen faith over submission to the GWC's false doctrine.

A brilliant light filled the cave. Zophiel materialized, wings folded close, face grave beneath his celestial helm.

"Their blood cries out from the ground," Enoch's voice cracked.

"They died as martyrs, sealed in their faith." Zophiel's voice carried both steel and sorrow. "But the time for gathering the remnant has passed. Those who would choose truth have made their choice."

The angel unfurled a dark cloak that seemed woven from shadows themselves. "The GWC has cemented its power. They've rejected every warning, every chance for repentance. Now judgment must fall."

Enoch ran his fingers across the cloth. It rippled like water under his touch, yet felt solid as armor. "The plagues..."

"Yes. You must pronounce them, one by one." Zophiel draped the cloak around Enoch's shoulders. The hood settled over his head, obscuring his features in darkness. "Let those who rejected Yahweh's mercy taste His justice."

"So many will suffer." Enoch's heart ached at the thought.

"They chose their path when they took the Mark and bowed to false worship." Zophiel's wings spread, filling the cave with divine light. "Remember who you serve. Remember why you were called from paradise to this broken world."

The cloak seemed to pulse against Enoch's skin, humming with holy power. He thought of the believers gunned down while singing hymns, their bodies left to rot in the sun as warnings to others. His grief hardened into resolve.

"I am ready." He gripped his staff, feeling its ancient power resonate with his new garment. "Where shall I begin?"

"the city of Angels," Zophiel replied.

CHAPTER 14

The sun baked the cracked asphalt of the abandoned highway as Enoch walked south. His new cloak rippled in the hot wind, the hood casting deep shadows across his face despite the harsh daylight. A shimmer in the air caught his attention - the familiar presence of divine guidance pulling him toward a rusted pickup truck parked beneath a billboard.

A man sat in the truck's bed, Bible open on his lap, muttering to himself as he traced lines of text with his finger. Sweat darkened his collar, and frustration creased his brow.

"What troubles you, brother?" Enoch approached the vehicle.

The man startled, nearly dropping his Bible. "These prophecies... I can't make sense of them. The Mark, the beast, the angels' messages..." He shook his head. "My congregation looks to me for answers, but I have none."

"Show me what you're reading." Enoch climbed into the truck bed, the metal groaning under his weight.

"Revelation 14." The preacher pointed to the verses. "Three angels with messages for the world. But what do they mean in these times?"

Enoch traced the familiar words. "The first angel carries the everlasting gospel, calling all to worship the Creator and keep His commandments - including His Sabbath."

"But the Green World Church says-"

"The second angel announces Babylon's fall - the collapse of false religious systems that have merged with earthly powers."

The preacher's eyes widened as understanding dawned.

"And the third warns against receiving the Mark of the Beast - a sign of allegiance to man's laws over God's." Enoch's voice carried the weight of divine authority. "Those who keep God's commandments and hold fast to Jesus' testimony will stand through the coming trials."

"The Green Mark..." The preacher's hand trembled as he touched his unmarked wrist. "They're pressuring everyone to take it. Calling it salvation for the planet."

"It's a choice between God's seal and man's Mark. Between true worship and false religion."

The preacher closed his Bible, determination replacing confusion. "I must warn my people."

"There's more you should know." Enoch's voice dropped lower. "The GWC has issued new decrees. They've labeled the Commandment Keepers as terrorists. Death warrants await those who speak against their Mark."

The preacher's face paled. "Death warrants?"

"The massacre in Las Vegas was just the beginning. They hunt us now, brother. Your congregation needs wisdom more than boldness. Share truth in whispers, in homes, one heart at a time."

"Like the early church during Roman persecution." The preacher clutched his Bible closer. "We'll meet in secret, use symbols to identify fellow believers."

"The Holy Spirit will guide you. Look for the cloud by day, the pillar of fire by night. God hasn't abandoned His people."

The preacher nodded, his expression hardening with resolve. "Thank you, stranger. Your words have-" He turned to face Enoch, but the truck bed sat empty. The metal hadn't even creaked with departure.

The hot wind whipped dust across the empty highway. No footprints marked the ground where Enoch had stood moments before. Only the lingering sense of divine presence assured the preacher he hadn't imagined the encounter.

* * *

Inside the dimly lit cathedral, rows of wooden pews creaked beneath the weight of the faithful. Stained glass windows cast colored shadows across stone floors as incense curled through shafts of morning light. Father Michael stood at the altar, his weathered hands trembling as he prepared for Sun day mass.

A flash of white light filled the sanctuary. When it faded, Enoch stood before the congregation, his presence commanding immediate silence.

"Your devotion is genuine," Enoch's voice echoed off the vaulted ceiling. "But you worship on the wrong day."

Father Michael stepped forward. "Who are you to-"

"The first angel's message rings clear - worship Him who made heaven and earth." Enoch raised his staff. "The Creator blessed and sanctified the seventh day, not the first."

"But the Church teaches-"

"Men changed God's times and laws. The second angel warns of Babylon's fall - false teachings that lead God's people astray." Enoch moved down the center aisle. "The third angel speaks of a choice - between God's seal and man's Mark."

An elderly woman in the front pew clutched her rosary. "The Green Mark... we refused it."

"You showed wisdom there." Enoch nodded. "But true worship requires full obedience. The Sabbath stands as God's eternal sign."

Father Michael sank to his knees, tears streaming down his face. "All these years... we've been wrong?"

A warm breeze swept through the church, though no windows were open. The Holy Spirit's presence filled the sanctuary, touching hearts and opening minds. Members of the congregation began to weep, others raised their hands in prayer.

"The Spirit confirms this truth," Father Michael whispered. "Brothers and sisters, we must reform our ways."

The congregation murmured in agreement, the Holy Spirit's conviction clear on their faces. Their Sunday traditions, held for generations, crumbled before divine truth.

"Keep God's commandments," Enoch said. "All of them. The time of testing approaches."

Father Michael turned back to Enoch, questions burning on his lips - but the mysterious figure had vanished. The spot where he'd stood moments before was empty, no trace remaining of his presence except the lingering scent of morning dew and mountain air.

Several congregants gasped. An altar boy dropped his brass candlestick with a clang that echoed through the sanctuary. The elderly woman with the rosary crossed herself, muttering prayers under her breath.

"Like the angels of old," Father Michael breathed, touching the spot where Enoch had stood. The stone floor felt cool and ordinary beneath his fingers. "He appeared with God's message, then departed just as swiftly."

The morning sun streamed through the stained glass windows, painting the empty space with prismatic colors where the stranger had delivered his powerful message about the Sabbath truth. The incense smoke curled through these beams, but no longer seemed to matter - the old traditions felt hollow now in the wake of divine revelation.

"Father," one deacon approached the altar, his voice shaking. "What do we do now?"

The priest rose slowly from his knees, newfound purpose straightening his shoulders. The Holy Spirit's presence remained thick in the air, a testament that the supernatural encounter had been real. "We must spread the word in these last days so that others can be warned before they receive the Mark of the Beast," the Priest said.

* * *

Saul paced across the polished marble floor of the GWC headquarters war room. Digital screens covered the walls, displaying surveillance footage from every major city. Red dots marked confirmed sightings of Commandment Keepers.

"These religious zealots mock everything we've built." His fist slammed against the steel conference table. "Their defiance spreads like a virus."

The assembled military commanders shifted in their seats. General Chen cleared his throat. "Our forces are ready. Twenty thousand troops, backed by the latest combat drones and surveillance tech."

"Double it." Saul's eyes narrowed. "I want them found. Every last one."

"Sir, that's more firepower than most nations-"

"They have supernatural help." Saul jabbed a finger at the footage showing Enoch vanishing from the cathedral. "We need overwhelming force. Send the order - anyone harboring Commandment Keepers will face immediate execution."

Screens flickered as orders transmitted across the global network. Within minutes, armored vehicles rolled through city streets. Helicopters thundered overhead, searchlights cutting through the night. Teams in tactical gear broke down doors, dragging families from their homes.

"Sir, first reports coming in." An aide handed Saul a tablet. "Three hundred arrested in Seoul. Eight hundred in Mumbai. Over a thousand in São Paulo."

Saul's lips curved into a bitter smile. "Excellent. Send them all to the re-education camps. Break their will. Make examples of the leaders."

"What about the children?"

"Separate them. Young minds are easier to reshape." Saul turned to face the window, watching troop carriers stream out of the military base below. "The time for tolerance is over. Either they accept the Mark and our authority, or they face extinction."

The hunt had begun. Across the globe, Saul's army descended upon the faithful with mechanized precision. Steel-toed boots kicked in doors. Rifles pointed at kneeling parents. Children screamed as they were torn from their mothers' arms.

A new dark age had dawned, just as the prophecy foretold. The dragon made war against those who kept the commandments of God.

CHAPTER 15

The sea breeze carried salt and diesel fumes across the San Pedro docks. Enoch materialized between stacked shipping containers, his hooded cloak rippling in the wind. The port sprawled before him - cranes reaching toward the sky like metal giants, cargo ships dotting the harbor.

People emerged from shadows and doorways. First a handful, then dozens, then hundreds. They moved with purpose but kept to the edges of buildings, away from security cameras and drone patrols. Many wore simple clothes Marked with discrete crosses or fish symbols.

"The time has come." Enoch's voice carried across the gathering crowd. "You've remained faithful despite persecution. Despite the Mark being forced upon society."

A woman clutched her children closer. "They took my husband last week. The camps-"

"The camps cannot hold back God's truth." Enoch raised his staff. "Just as Pharaoh's armies couldn't stop the Exodus, these modern pharaohs will fail."

The crowd swelled to thousands, filling the spaces between containers and warehouses. They came from all walks of life - dock workers still in coveralls, office workers in wrinkled suits, families with small children. All bore the haunted looks of those who'd seen too much suffering.

"The plagues have begun," Enoch continued. "The sores that afflict Mark-bearers are just the start. God's judgment falls on those who chose the GWC's false worship."

Murmurs rippled through the assembly. Many nodded, having witnessed the plague's effects firsthand.

"But you've kept His commandments. Remembered His Sabbath. Refused to bow to man's laws over God's." Enoch swept his arm across the crowd. "You are the remnant He promised would stand in these last days."

A young man stepped forward. "What should we do? The armies are everywhere."

"Stand firm in your faith. Help each other. The time of trouble grows darker, but remember - after Egypt's plagues came deliverance."

The multitude pressed closer, hungry for hope, for guidance, for confirmation that their sacrifices meant something. Despite the risk of gathering, they stayed - thousands of faithful waiting to hear more about the prophecies unfolding before them.

Floodlights blazed across the docks. Armored vehicles rolled in from every direction, their engines drowning out the sea breeze. Saul emerged from the lead vehicle, his pristine GWC uniform stark against the gritty port backdrop.

"Surround them. No one leaves." Saul's voice crackled through megaphones. "The terrorist calling himself 'Enoch' ends his reign of terror tonight."

Armed troops formed a perimeter, weapons trained on the crowd. Helicopter rotors thundered overhead, searchlights sweeping across frightened faces.

"Your false prophet has led you to destruction." Saul raised his hand. "Surrender him, and you may fell the mercy of reeducation."

Enoch stepped forward, staff planted firmly. "The Lord parts waters for His people."

The crowd surged toward the wilderness beyond the port. As GWC forces moved to intercept, shipping containers toppled like dominoes, blocking their path. Chaos erupted - shots fired, screams echoing off the metal walls, but the believers slipped through gaps and shadows.

"After them!" Saul's face contorted with rage.

Enoch stood at the harbor's edge, alone now. The water lapped at his feet as Saul's forces closed in.

"Your armies cannot stop what comes next." Enoch struck the water with his staff. "As in Moses' time, the waters turn to blood."

The sea rippled, then churned. Red spread like ink through water, starting at the point of impact and racing outward. Fish floated to the surface, lifeless. The stench of death rose as the crimson tide spread across the harbor.

Saul staggered back. "What have you done?"

"This is no chemical attack or terrorist plot." Enoch's voice carried over the lapping of blood-water. "This is the second plague. God's judgment falls on those who persecute His people."

The bloody water stretched to the horizon, dead sea life bobbing in the crimson waves. Fishing boats listed in the thickening liquid as their crews abandoned ship.

The harbor's crimson waters lapped against concrete walls, their metallic stench filling the air. Saul's forces surrounded Enoch, their weapons trained on his cloaked figure.

"Take him." Saul's command cut through the eerie silence.

Two soldiers rushed forward. Their hands passed through empty air as Enoch vanished, leaving only footprints in the blood-soaked ground. The troops spun, weapons sweeping the area.

"Find him!" Saul kicked a dead fish from his path. "Search every container, every warehouse."

A flash of movement caught his eye. Enoch stood atop a crane, his cloak billowing against the night sky. The soldiers opened fire, bullets sparking off metal where the figure had been moments before.

"Sir, he's by the main gate!" A soldier pointed his rifle toward the port entrance.

Enoch appeared and disappeared across the docks, always just beyond their reach. Each time he vanished, more soldiers lowered their weapons, faces pale in the emergency lights.

"It's not possible," one whispered, backing away.

"Stand your ground!" Saul grabbed the soldier's collar. "He's using tricks, holograms-"

"Like the plague is a trick?" The soldier gestured at the harbor. "Like the sores were a trick?"

More troops broke ranks, their training crumbling before events they couldn't explain. Saul watched his carefully constructed authority dissolving like salt in the blood-red sea.

Enoch materialized beside him. "Your armies cannot fight what comes from above."

Saul swung, his fist passing through the air. He stumbled, catching himself against a shipping container. When he looked up, Enoch stood at the water's edge again.

"The plagues will continue," Enoch's voice carried across the docks. "Until all see the truth about the Mark and the GWC's deception."

The blood-red waters of San Pedro harbor churned beneath the night sky. Saul slumped against a container, his pristine uniform now splattered with crimson droplets. His radio crackled with reports of mass desertions across the port.

"Sir, we've lost contact with the eastern perimeter." An aide approached, keeping his distance from the contaminated water. "Half the containment force is gone."

Saul yanked off his GWC insignia and hurled it into the bloody surf. The metal badge sank beneath the surface with a soft plop. He'd built his career on order, on control, on the promise that the Green World Church could protect humanity from chaos. Now that order crumbled around him.

"Get me a secure line to headquarters." Saul straightened his jacket. "And find someone who can explain this... phenomenon."

The aide hesitated. "The scientists who examined the staff, sir. They're still in the medical ward. The blindness hasn't improved."

Across the harbor, fish continued surfacing - their silver scales dulled by death. The stench grew stronger as the night wore on, driving even the most hardened troops back from the waterline. Emergency crews arrived wearing hazmat suits, taking samples of the transformed water.

Through it all, Enoch's words echoed in Saul's mind: "Until all see the truth." He'd dismissed the man as a terrorist, a clever manipulator using technology to create illusions. But as he watched the harbor's waters turn to blood, doubt gnawed at his certainty.

The radio squawked again. "Sir, reports coming in. The contamination is spreading. Every harbor, every port... it's all turning red."

Saul stared at his reflection in the bloody water. The face that looked back seemed older, haunted. He remembered the sores that had plagued Mark-bearers, the fire that consumed the stadium and his men, how they'd struck only those bearing the GWC's symbol. The truth he'd fought so hard to suppress bubbled up like the dead fish around him.

What if they'd been wrong? What if the GWC's path wasn't humanity's salvation but its damnation?

Saul wiped the sweat from his brow, his moment of doubt evaporating like morning dew. Years of GWC conditioning reasserted themselves. He'd dedicated his life to maintaining order, to building a unified world under one faith. These commandment keepers threatened everything they'd built.

"No more hesitation." Saul grabbed his radio. "All units fall back to LAX. We'll coordinate from there."

The remaining troops loaded into their vehicles, tires splashing through puddles of blood-water as they retreated from the harbor. Saul sat rigid in the lead vehicle, his jaw clenched. The drive to LAX passed in tense silence, broken only by status updates from other GWC forces.

They pulled into the airport's military wing. Aircraft sat ready on the tarmac, their engines idling. Technicians had transformed the main terminal into a command center, screens displaying surveillance feeds from across the city.

"I want drones in the air." Saul strode through the terminal, issuing rapid-fire commands. "Focus on the desert regions first. These believers always flee to the wilderness."

"Sir, what about the... incidents?" An officer gestured at the footage of the harbor.

"Tricks and terrorism, nothing more." Saul's voice hardened. The GWC will be filled with God and Mother Earth. We must eliminate the heretical commandment keepers.

He traced a line across the tactical map. "Set up checkpoints here, here, and here. No one passes without Mark verification. Deploy the hunter-killer teams in groups of four. Shoot on sight."

The command center hummed with activity as orders went out. Saul watched the pieces fall into place, his earlier doubts buried under layers of righteous certainty. He'd hunt these believers to the ends of the earth if necessary.

"The one world church will prevail," he whispered, touching the Mark on his hand. "God wills it."

The Hollywood sign loomed against the smog-filled sky, its white letters dulled by years of pollution. Enoch materialized beneath the iconic landmark, his cloak settling around him as the sea breeze carried the scent of blood from the harbors below.

A flash of light pierced the haze. Zophiel stood before him, the angel's form shifting between human and divine, impossible to focus on directly.

"The waters run red with judgment." Zophiel's voice resonated with both masculine and feminine tones. "But your work here isn't finished."

Enoch leaned on his staff, watching emergency vehicles snake through the streets below. "The believers fled into the wilderness."

"As they must. The desert will shelter them, as it sheltered God's people before." Zophiel touched Enoch's shoulder. "You've shown them the way. Now you must return to New Eden."

"The remnant church grows stronger." Enoch traced the path ahead in his mind - through canyons and valleys, past GWC checkpoints and drone patrols.

"Their faith will be tested further." Zophiel's form flickered. "The plagues continue, but you've prepared them. Go now. The journey is long, but the path will open before you."

The angel vanished, leaving Enoch alone on the hillside. He pulled his hood lower and started north, his staff marking each step toward the hidden sanctuary of New Eden. The city sprawled behind him, its waters turned to blood, while ahead lay miles of desert and the faithful who awaited his return. A lone church bell rang in the distance.

CHAPTER 16

Saul sat alone in his office at LAX, staring at the Mark on his hand. The green symbol pulsed faintly in the dim light, a constant reminder of his dedication to the GWC. Photos and reports scattered across his desk showed the devastation - harbors filled with blood, the stadium's ashes, countless Mark-bearers suffering from sores.

His fingers traced the scar on his temple where shrapnel had struck during the stadium incident. The memory of that day haunted him - the sudden flash, the screams, his men vaporized in holy fire. Only those without the Mark had walked away unscathed.

"Everything I believed..." He picked up a photo of himself at his GWC initiation, younger and certain of his path. Back then, the choice seemed clear - unite humanity under one faith, one purpose. The Mark had promised prosperity, peace, an end to religious division.

Across the city, Enoch paused atop a hill overlooking the sprawling metropolis. His staff cast long shadows in the setting sun as he considered the souls below. Three thousand years with the Divine had shown him humanity's endless cycle of pride and fall, yet his heart ached for those trapped in the GWC's deception.

The weight of his mission pressed upon him. Not just to guide the faithful, but to witness humanity's final choice between truth and convenience. The plagues would continue, each judgment revealing the Mark for what it truly was - not salvation, but bondage.

He touched the spot where Zophiel had Marked him with the seal of God. Unlike the GWC's Mark, this divine signature carried no earthly power or privilege. It offered only truth and the path of righteousness.

"The harvest approaches," he whispered, remembering countless souls he'd guided through the ages. Some had chosen light, others darkness. Now, in these last days, each person would make their eternal decision.

The night wrapped Los Angeles in an unnatural stillness. Enoch knelt in prayer on the rooftop of an abandoned church, his staff laid across his lap. The stars above had changed position since his time with the Divine - a reminder of how long he'd been away from that realm of pure light.

A cool breeze stirred his cloak, carrying the scent of ash and decay. His eyes closed as fragments of memory washed over him: the celestial courts, the ancient prophecies, the warnings of what was to come.

"The seventh seal approaches." Zophiel materialized beside him, wings folded against the darkness. "You remember what was written?"

"When the Lamb opened the seventh seal," Enoch recited, "there was silence in heaven for about half an hour."

"The silence begins." Zophiel's voice carried an edge of urgency. "Look."

Enoch opened his eyes. Across the city, lights flickered and died in patches, section by section, like candles being snuffed out. The usual urban cacophony faded to whispers, then nothing. Even the wind held its breath.

"The plagues were just the beginning," Zophiel said. "What comes next will test even the faithful. Many will fall away when they see the price of truth."

In the distance, a lone church bell tolled - three deep rings that echoed through the empty streets. Enoch's staff hummed with energy, responding to something unseen.

"Three days," Zophiel whispered. "Three days until the silence breaks. Watch for the signs: a child will speak in tongues of fire, the waters will part once more, and those who bear the Mark will cry out for the mountains to fall upon them."

The angel's form faded. "Remember what you witnessed in the courts above. The end comes not with thunder, but with silence."

The silence shattered as emergency sirens wailed through Los Angeles. Red and blue lights painted the buildings while GWC security forces poured into the streets. Their vehicles bore the familiar green insignia, now glowing with an eerie phosphorescence in the darkness.

Enoch melted into the shadows of the church rooftop, his cloak rendering him nearly invisible. Below, squadrons of armed men swept building to building, their boots echoing on empty pavement.

"Clear the sector! Find the Stranger!" A commander's voice crackled over megaphones. "All citizens remain in your homes. This is a Level One manhunt."

Through gaps in the buildings, Enoch spotted massive spotlights being erected, their beams cutting through the night sky. Helicopters thundered overhead, their searchlights probing every corner and alley.

A group of soldiers burst through the church's front doors. Their boots pounded up stairs and through corridors. Enoch remained motionless as they emerged onto the roof, weapons raised.

"Sector Seven clear," one reported into his radio. "No sign of the target."

The soldier's Mark pulsed visibly on his right hand, an angry green that seemed to throb in time with his heartbeat. Fresh sores had erupted around his neck, weeping clear fluid that stained his collar.

"Sir, the sores are getting worse," another soldier whispered, scratching at his own Mark. "Medical says the treatments aren't working anymore."

"Keep it down," the commander snapped. "Focus on the mission. The Stranger will pay for what he's done to us."

They swept past Enoch's position without seeing him, their flashlight beams passing through the space where he stood. As their footsteps faded, he gripped his staff tighter. The wood thrummed with energy, responding to the growing darkness around him.

The city had become a web of searchlights and sirens, a net drawing ever tighter. But Enoch knew his path lay not in evasion, but in confrontation. The time for hiding was ending. As the soldiers disappeared down the stairwell, he stepped out of the shadows, staff raised toward the star-filled heavens.

***

In an abandoned warehouse on the outskirts of Los Angeles, Jose arranged medical supplies and provisions across folding tables. Former GWC members who'd removed their Marks huddled in small groups, tending to each other's wounds. The raw patches where they'd carved out the green symbols still oozed, but their eyes held a newfound clarity.

"The safe houses in Nevada are ready." Jose passed a stack of maps to a group of ex-military converts. "We'll move in groups of three, using the old logging roads."

A woman with graying hair sorted through bottles of antibiotics. "What about those still trapped in the re-education camps?"

Enoch has a plan. Jose touched the spot where the GWC had tortured him, leaving a burn mark. We need everyone ready to move when the signal comes.

Across the city, in the gleaming GWC LAX headquarters, Saul paced before a wall of monitors. Each screen showed different angles of the city - thermal imaging, satellite feeds, drone footage. Red dots marked confirmed sightings of the Stranger.

"The special forces teams are in position." A lieutenant pointed to clusters of green indicators. "We've changed their weapons with hallow point ammunition, as requested."

Saul traced the pattern of sightings. "And the new Mark enhancement?"

"Ready for deployment." The lieutenant held up a syringe filled with luminescent green fluid. "Once injected, it should prevent the sores and strengthen the connection."

"Begin the procedures immediately. I want every soldier enhanced before dawn." Saul pressed his palm against a scanner, and his Mark flared with intense light. "This time, the Stranger won't slip away."

***

In a hidden chamber beneath an old church, Zophiel appeared to Enoch. "More gather to the truth each hour. The faithful hide them in caves, just as in days of old."

"And those who hunt us grow stronger," Enoch replied, watching through a narrow window as GWC patrols passed.

"They forge their weapons of flesh and steel," Zophiel said, "while you have gathered warriors of spirit and truth. The final battle approaches, but not as they expect."

Enoch found Jose in the warehouse's makeshift infirmary, bent over a young woman whose Mark removal had become infected. The former GWC officer's hands shook as he cleaned the wound.

"The antibiotics aren't working anymore." Jose's voice cracked. "Each day, more people want their Marks removed, but the procedures keep failing. I can't save them all."

"You carry too much weight, my friend." Enoch placed a hand on Jose's shoulder.

Jose jerked away. "And you carry too little. Where were you when they raided the safe house in Pasadena? Fifteen dead, including children."

"I go where I am directed-"

"Directed?" Jose slammed down a medical tray. "While you follow your divine signs, real people suffer. We need more than prophecies and miracles. We need protection, resources, an actual plan."

The woman on the cot whimpered. Jose immediately softened his voice, returning to dress her wounds. "I believe in what you stand for, Enoch. But faith alone won't stop Saul's armies."

"You think I don't feel their pain?" Enoch's staff hummed with suppressed energy. "Every soul lost tears at me. But if I deviate from my purpose, if I let human wisdom override divine guidance-"

"Then what? The world ends?" Jose's bitter laugh echoed through the warehouse. "It's already ending. Look around. While you chase your visions, Saul grows stronger. His enhanced soldiers control the city. Soon there won't be anywhere left to hide."

Enoch studied his friend's face - the deep lines of exhaustion, the haunted eyes of someone who'd seen too much suffering. Jose had sacrificed everything to help the resistance, yet each setback seemed to chip away at his conviction.

"Perhaps..." Jose's voice dropped to a whisper. "Perhaps we were wrong. Not about the Mark being evil, but about fighting it. How many more have to die before we accept that we can't win?"

The words hung between them like a physical barrier. For the first time since awakening in this age, Enoch felt truly alone.

Enoch raised his staff, the wood pulsing with divine energy. "Your doubt speaks from weariness, not truth. Remember what you witnessed at the stadium?"

"Miracles and destruction." Jose slumped against a supply crate. "But Saul's forces grow stronger each day. The enhanced Mark gives them powers we can't match."

A commotion erupted near the warehouse entrance. Three figures stumbled in, supporting a fourth who writhed in agony. Green light pulsed from the Mark on his forehead, spreading luminescent tendrils across his skin.

"Found him outside the perimeter," one of the resistance fighters called. "Says he's a GWC deserter. The enhancement is rejecting."

Jose rushed to help, but Enoch blocked his path. The staff's glow intensified as he approached the suffering man.

"The enhancement..." The deserter's voice came in gasps. "Saul said it would protect us. Make us stronger. But it's changing us. Not just our bodies."

Enoch knelt beside him. The enhanced Mark blazed like toxic fire, consuming the man from within. But beneath the artificial light, Enoch saw something else - a deeper corruption taking root.

"Your thoughts," Enoch said. "They're not entirely your own anymore, are they?"

The deserter's eyes widened. "How did you... The voices. They started after the injection. Commands. Urges. At first, we thought it was just the neural link to headquarters."

"What kind of commands?" Jose asked.

"Hunt. Kill. Destroy the unfaithful." Tears streaked the deserter's face. "I couldn't... couldn't keep following them. But the others..

. they're embracing it. The enhancement isn't just controlling our bodies."

Enoch placed his hand on the man's forehead. The staff's light pulsed once, and the green tendrils receded slightly. The deserter's breathing steadied.

"Now you understand," Enoch said to Jose. "This was never a battle of weapons and armies. The Mark's true purpose reveals itself - not just control of the body, but corruption of the soul."

Jose stared at the deserter, watching the green tendrils pulse beneath his skin. The man's revelation about the enhanced Mark struck deeper than any physical wound.

"The voices..." The deserter clutched his head. "They're getting stronger. Saul's connected to all of us now. He sees through our eyes, whispers in our thoughts."

Enoch's staff glowed brighter, its light forming a protective barrier around the suffering man. The warehouse's shadows danced across the concrete walls as other resistance members gathered closer, drawn by the divine radiance.

"Each enhancement binds them tighter to Saul's will," Enoch said. "The Mark was always more than a symbol - it's becoming a hive mind, corrupting and consuming."

A woman stepped forward. The scar where she'd removed her Mark was still fresh. "That's why the removal procedures keep failing. The enhanced version... it's not just on the skin anymore. It's in their blood, their minds."

"We found entire units of enhanced soldiers moving in perfect synchronization," another fighter added. "No radio commands, no hand signals. Like they shared one consciousness."

The deserter convulsed, green light flaring from his Mark. "He knows I'm here. Saul... he's trying to pull me back. The others are coming."

Enoch pressed his staff against the ground. Divine energy rippled outward in concentric circles, washing over the gathered resistance members. The warehouse fell silent except for the deserter's labored breathing.

"The enemy isn't flesh and blood," Enoch said, his voice carrying to every corner of the space. "Saul's enhanced army is becoming something beyond human. But remember - no power of man can stand against divine truth."

Jose touched his own burnt scar, understanding finally dawning in his eyes. "That's why you haven't confronted Saul directly. This isn't about defeating his forces..."

"It's about saving souls," Enoch finished. "One heart at a time, before they're lost completely."

Gather all that remains and get word to the others, we must make our way to New Eden at once.

CHAPTER 17

The GWC recon sniper team lay prone beneath thermal blankets, their enhanced optics scanning the valley below. New Eden sprawled across the desert floor - a sprawling compound of tents and makeshift structures. The setting sun cast long shadows across the settlement, but their augmented vision pierced through the growing darkness.

"Multiple heat signatures," Lieutenant David Gleen whispered, his enhanced Mark pulsing green beneath his tactical gear. "Concentrate on the central structure. Looks like some kind of gathering."

Sergeant Torres adjusted his scope, the neural interface from his Mark, feeding tactical data directly to his consciousness. "I count at least two hundred. No perimeter defenses that I can see. They're not even trying to hide."

"Overconfident." Gleens' finger tapped his rifle. "Or they know something we don't."

The third member of their team, Private Wu, remained silent as he established a secure neural link to the GWC command. His enhanced Mark flared briefly as the connection engaged.

"Target location confirmed," Wu transmitted through the neural network. "Settlement designated 'New Eden' houses approximately three thousand subjects. Minimal defenses. Awaiting instructions."

The response came instantly, flooding their shared consciousness with new orders. Gleen's Mark burned brighter as the commands integrated with his thoughts.

"Maintain observation," he relayed to his team. "Command wants eyes on any movement. They're mobilizing strike teams from three surrounding sectors."

Torres shifted position, his enhanced vision zooming in on the settlement's main entrance. "Movement at the gate. Single figure in a hooded cloak."

"Facial recognition?" Gleen asked.

"Negative. Some kind of interference." Torres frowned. "The enhancement can't get a lock on the target."

Wu's Mark pulsed erratically. "Sir, something's wrong with the neural feed. Getting scattered readings..."

The hooded figure below raised what appeared to be a wooden staff. Even from their elevated position, the snipers felt a wave of energy wash over them. Their enhanced Marks flared painfully.

"Neural link's destabilizing," Wu gasped. "Can't maintain connection to command."

Chen tried to steady his rifle, but his hands trembled as the enhancement in his blood reacted to the unknown energy. "Hold position. We need to-"

The shot cracked through the evening air. Jose's body crumpled mid-stride, the hood falling back to reveal his face frozen in surprise. Blood pooled beneath him, staining the desert sand crimson.

"Target down," Torres reported, his enhanced vision confirming the kill.

But something was wrong. The hooded figure's collapse had triggered chaos in the compound below, yet their Marks burned with increasing intensity. Static filled their neural feeds.

"Secondary target emerging," Gleen called out. Through his scope, he tracked another cloaked figure striding from the main building. This one moved with purpose, staff raised high.

The figure's hood fell back. Enoch's face blazed with righteous anger as he knelt beside Jose's body. The staff in his hands pulsed with blinding light.

"Neural link critical," Wu choked out. His Mark flared painfully, sending sparks of agony through his skull. "Can't... maintain..."

The sniper team's enhanced vision systems were overloaded, leaving them blind in the growing darkness. Their Marks burned like brands against their skin.

"Fall back," Gleen ordered, but his commands couldn't penetrate the static flooding their neural network. The enhancement that had made them elite soldiers now threatened to tear them apart from within.

Below, Enoch's voice carried across the valley with supernatural clarity: "The blood of the faithful cries out from the ground. As Cain was marked, so shall you bear witness."

Torres clawed at his ark as it seared deeper into his flesh. "Sir, we need to-"

A column of light erupted from Enoch's staff, illuminating the valley like a second sun. The sniper team's screams were lost in the overwhelming brightness as their enhanced bodies betrayed them, their Marks becoming instruments of judgment rather than power.

Through the chaos, Jose's blood continued to seep into the desert soil, each drop a testament to the escalating war between ancient faith and modern corruption.

Enoch knelt beside Jose's lifeless form, his friend's blood soaking into the desert sand. The staff thrummed with divine energy in his grip as memories of his time with Yahshua flooded back - the power of resurrection, the triumph of life over death.

He placed his hand on Jose's chest, still warm despite the growing chill of evening. The bullet wound gaped angry and red, but Enoch saw past the physical damage to the spark of life that lingered. He wept.

"My friend, your work is not finished." Enoch's voice carried the weight of heaven's authority. "In the name of Yahshua, who conquered death itself, rise."

The staff blazed with blinding light. Divine energy pulsed through Enoch's arm and into Jose's body. The blood that had spilled now flow backward, defying natural law as it returned to Jose's veins. Muscle and tissue knit together, the bullet pushing out and falling harmlessly to the sand.

Jose's eyes snapped open. He drew in a sharp breath as color returned to his face. His hand flew to his chest, finding smooth skin where the wound had been.

"Brother Enoch?" Jose pushed himself up on his elbows, looking around in confusion. "I was... I thought..."

"Death has no power here." Enoch helped Jose to his feet. "The enemy sought to silence you, but God has other plans."

Jose stood steady, stronger than before. The experience had left its mark - not in his flesh, but in his eyes. They held a new fire, a deeper understanding of the power they served.

"The snipers..." Jose glanced toward the ridge where the GWC team had been positioned.

"They witnessed God's power. Whether they choose to accept or deny it, they will carry that truth with them."

A warm glow emanated from Jose's forehead, pulsing in rhythm with his heartbeat. He lifted his hand to touch the spot, feeling divine energy coursing through his body. The Mark of God shimmered with an ethereal light, identical to the one Enoch bore.

"This feeling..." Jose's voice trembled with awe. "It's like being filled with pure light."

Enoch placed a steadying hand on Jose's shoulder. "The seal of the living God. You've been chosen, just as the faithful were Marked in Jerusalem long ago."

The Mark continued to radiate, casting soft golden light across Jose's features. His entire countenance had transformed - where there had been weariness, now there was strength. Where doubt had lingered, certainty took root.

"I understand now," Jose said, his eyes clear and focused. "What you've been showing us, what we're fighting for - it's all so much clearer."

The staff in Enoch's hand hummed in harmony with both their Marks, creating a resonance that seemed to push back the encroaching darkness. The divine seal on their foreheads stood in stark contrast to the GWC's Mark - one brought life and clarity, the other bondage and corruption.

"The Mark is both protection and purpose," Enoch explained. "It sets us apart from those who've chosen to follow the beast's system."

Jose straightened, a new purpose clear in his bearing. The Mark of God had transformed him from a follower into a fellow witness, Marked by heaven itself, for the work ahead.

Inside New Eden's central chamber, converted from an old school bus, Enoch guided a group of twenty believers through ancient Hebrew scriptures. Scrolls and digital tablets lay scattered across wooden tables, bridging millennia of sacred knowledge.

"The faith in your hearts carries divine authority," Enoch traced symbols in the air with his staff. "But authority requires wisdom to wield it properly."

Jose moved between the study groups, his newly gained Mark gleaming. "Brother Steven, show me again how you're reading that passage."

A former GWC data analyst looked up from his tablet. "I'm cross-referencing the original Hebrew with modern translations. There are patterns here - connections between ancient prophecies and current events."

Enoch nodded approvingly. "The Holy Spirit grants understanding, but we must also train our minds. The enemy has technology and weapons. We have something far more powerful - truth."

The chamber hummed with focused energy as believers practiced channeling divine power through prayer and meditation. Some worked with simple wooden staves, learning the principles that made Enoch's rod a conduit for heavenly authority.

"Remember," Enoch demonstrated a motion that sent ripples of light through the air, "these are not magical tools. They amplify the faith already within you."

In another corner, Jose led a group practicing Krav-Maga,

"Focus on the strength of faith to guide your movements," Jose instructed. "Let it anchor you when they try to attack"

A young woman raised her hand. "But what about their enhanced soldiers? The ones with augmented strength?"

"Physical power means nothing against spiritual authority," Enoch replied. "David faced Goliath with five stones and unwavering faith. We face our giants with the same conviction."

The training continued as the sunset, each believer growing stronger in their understanding and abilities. They weren't building an army - they were becoming witnesses, equipped with both ancient wisdom and divine power to stand against the coming storm.

Enoch stood atop New Eden's highest point, his staff casting long shadows in the desert twilight. Below, the compound buzzed with purposeful activity as the faithful prepared for what lay ahead. The Mark of God on his forehead pulsed with increasing frequency - a divine warning of approaching conflict.

Jose approached, carrying ancient scrolls mixed with tactical data stripped from GWC systems. "Their forces are mobilizing across three sectors. Neural-enhanced troops, automated weapons platforms, enhanced microwave crowd control."

"They gather armies of flesh and metal," Enoch traced patterns in the dust with his staff. "While we gather the weapons of spirit and truth."

Inside the main cave, believers moved with quiet efficiency. Some transcribed prophecies onto hardened data crystals that could survive electromagnetic attacks. Others memorized the text from the worn leather Bible.

"The GWC thinks this is about territory or control," Jose spread out a map marked with enemy positions. "They don't understand we're fighting for souls, not land."

Enoch's Mark flared as he sensed ripples of divine energy flowing through the compound. In different sections, the faithful had organized into specialized groups. Some focused on emergency first aid, others on defensive barriers. A few worked with Jose, learning to disrupt the neural networks that enslaved millions through the Mark of the Beast.

"Each according to their gifts," Enoch observed. "As it was in the early church, so it is now."

The staff in his hand hummed with increasing intensity. Around the compound, other wooden rods responded in harmony, creating a resonance that strengthened the faithful's connection to divine power. These simple tools, paired with unwavering faith, would stand against humanity's most advanced weapons.

"Brother Enoch," Jose's Mark pulsed in sync with the rising energy. "The outer teams report GWC dropships moving into position. They're establishing a perimeter."

"Then we continue our preparations," Enoch replied. "The time approaches when each must choose - the Mark of man's authority, or the seal of God's promise."

* * *

Saul burst through the polished obsidian doors of New Babylon's central command. His boots clicked against marble floors as he strode past rows of holographic displays tracking global movements. The Mark on his hand tingled - a reminder of his dedication to the GWC's cause.

"We found them." He spread detailed satellite imagery across Damien Folk's desk. "New Eden. Hidden in plain sight, using old mining roads and natural caverns."

Damien Folk rose from his chair, his tall frame casting a shadow across the tactical displays. The GWC president's cybernetic eye whirred as it processed the data. "How many?"

"Initial scans show several hundred. But their energy signatures are... unusual. Our sensors can't get clear readings."

"Then we'll send enough force to guarantee victory." Damien's metallic fingers traced patterns across the command console. "You'll lead five thousand of our best. Full tactical load-out, heavy weapons, air support."

Saul's Mark pulsed faster. "Five thousand? That's more than we've ever deployed for a single operation."

"This ends now." Damien's organic eye narrowed. "I want that compound reduced to ash. Every believer captured or eliminated. Their prophet's head on a pike."

"What about potential converts? Some might still accept the true Mark-"

"No more conversion attempts." Damien slammed his augmented fist on the desk. "They've rejected progress. Rejected unity. Gather your army, Saul. Show them the price of defiance."

Saul nodded, suppressing a flicker of doubt. He'd hunted believers before, but something about this operation felt different. The scale. The finality. The way his Mark burned when he looked at the surveillance footage of Enoch.

"I want you moving within six hours," Damien commanded. "Every combat-ready unit from the western seaboard. Full mechanized support. No survivors."

"It will be done." Saul turned to leave, already composing deployment orders in his neural link. Five thousand soldiers. Enough firepower to level a city. All to crush a group of religious refugees hiding in the desert.

CHAPTER 18

The first attack came at dawn. Three GWC gunships swooped low over the western outpost of New Eden, their rotors whipping up clouds of red desert sand. The handful of sentries barely had time to sound the alarm before plasma bolts scorched the surrounding earth.

"Get down!" Jose yanked a young lookout behind a boulder as enemy fire strafed their position. The boy's eyes went wide at the thunder of explosions, but his hands remained steady on his rifle.

The ships made another pass, this time dropping teams of GWC shock troops. Their black armor gleamed in the morning sun as they established a perimeter, methodically advancing toward the cave entrance.

"They're testing our defenses," Jose muttered into his comm unit. "Small force, probably looking for weak points." He counted at least twelve soldiers, all bearing the telltale green glow of the Mark on their hands.

The defenders held their positions, letting the GWC forces push forward. When the troops reached the first ring of boulders, hidden speakers crackled to life with the sound of ancient ram horn trumpets. Several soldiers stumbled, clutching their Marked hands as if burned.

"Now!" Jose's voice carried across the ravine. Defenders aimed from concealed positions, firing in short burst, their ancient rifles blessed by Enoch himself. The GWC troops found their advanced targeting systems scrambled, their plasma rifles sputtering and dying.

The skirmish lasted less than ten minutes. The gunships retreated, leaving their ground forces to withdraw in disarray. Only three defenders suffered minor injuries, while the attackers left behind damaged equipment and drops of blood in the sand.

Jose studied the abandoned GWC gear, his expression grim. This wasn't a serious attempt to breach their sanctuary - just a probe to test their strength and response time. The real assault would come soon, and it would be far worse than this morning's skirmish.

"Clean up and reinforce the positions," he ordered. "They'll be back, and next time they won't underestimate us."

***

On the eastern perimeter, Asher and Selene crouched behind the remains of an old water tower. The married couple - former GWC spies turned believers - recognized the tactical patterns of their old employers.

"Delta formation," Selene whispered, tracking movement through her binoculars. "They're using the old infiltration protocols."

Asher adjusted his grip on the simple wooden staff Enoch had blessed. "They changed the response codes last week. Our intel's already outdated."

A flash of green light pierced the pre-dawn gloom. GWC scouts materialized from their cloaking fields, their stealth suits humming with artificial power. The Mark on their hands pulsed in sync with their equipment.

"In His name," Asher breathed. He raised the staff and struck it against the ground three times. The impact sent ripples through the earth, disrupting the scouts' stealth fields. Their forms flickered and solidified, exposed in the open.

Selene touched the silver cross at her throat - not a religious symbol, but a sophisticated jamming device crafted by the New Eden engineers and blessed by Enoch. Static crackled across the GWC communication frequencies.

"Remember who we were," she called out to the scouts, her voice carrying across the rocky terrain. "And what made us choose differently?"

The scouts hesitated. One of them - a woman with sergeant's stripes - took a halting step forward. The Mark on her hand flared painfully, but she kept moving.

"The sores," she said. "They're getting worse, aren't they? The 'cure' isn't working anymore."

"There's another way," Asher responded. He lowered his staff. "We found healing. Real healing."

Two more scouts stepped forward, their weapons lowered. The sergeant reached up and removed her tactical helmet, revealing skin marred by the telltale lesions of the first plague.

"Show us," she said.

The remaining scouts melted back into the shadows, but Asher and Selene knew they'd be back - next time seeking truth rather than combat. They led the three defectors into the sanctuary, where Enoch waited to welcome more lost children home.

In the heart of New Eden's sanctuary, beneath weathered stone arches, the survivors gathered around flickering oil lamps. The air hung thick with incense and quiet prayers. Converts old and new filled the chamber - former GWC soldiers, desert wanderers, and those who'd carried the truth through generations of persecution.

Enoch stood at the center, his presence drawing every eye. The lamplight cast his shadow across cave paintings that depicted humanity's second exodus. His staff gleamed with an inner light that pulsed in rhythm with the believers' hearts.

"Each of us carries a different wound," Enoch's voice echoed off the stone. "But we share one purpose."

Jose stepped forward, rolling up his sleeve to reveal burn scars from GWC interrogators. "They took my family when I refused the Mark. But here, I found a new one."

The former GWC sergeant who'd defected that morning touched the lesions on her face. "We were promised paradise through technology and unity. Instead, we got slavery and pain."

"The Mark promised prosperity," Asher added, clutching Selene's hand. "But it chained our souls."

One by one, they shared their stories. A mother hid her children in the mountains when the Green Laws were passed. A priest who'd watched his congregation embrace the Mark until only he remained. Young ones born into hiding, knowing only stories of the world before.

Their voices wove together, pain and hope intertwining. As each person spoke, Enoch touched his hand to their foreheads, leaving behind a cool gleam that spread through their bodies - not a Mark of ownership like the GWC's brand, but a blessing of freedom.

"We are not merely refugees," Enoch said. "We are witnesses to truth. Each scar, each loss, each moment of defiance, lights the path for others."

The gathered believers pressed closer, their shadows merging on the cave walls. Former enemies stood shoulder to shoulder, their old divisions dissolved in shared purpose. The air crackled with something beyond electricity - a power older than the GWC's technology, deeper than their artificial unity.

Enoch raised his staff, and silence fell across the chamber. The oil lamps flickered, casting dancing shadows on the ancient walls. A cool breeze swept through the underground sanctuary, carrying with it the scent of desert sage and morning dew.

"The time draws near," he said. His weathered face bore the peace of one who had walked with God, yet his eyes held the weight of coming tribulation. "Our brothers and sisters still trapped within the GWC's walls need us now more than ever."

Jose stepped forward, his boots scraping against the stone floor. "The northern sectors reported increased patrols. They're scanning for unauthorized gatherings, using the new quantum detection grids."

"Let them search." Enoch's staff pulsed with inner light. "Their technology cannot pierce the veil of divine protection."

A young woman emerged from the crowd, her GWC tactical uniform stripped of rank insignias. "The enforcement divisions are changing their protocols. President Folk has authorized lethal force against any suspected Commandment Keepers."

Murmurs rippled through the gathering. Some clutched simple wooden crosses, others touched the scars where their Marks had once been.

"We've intercepted their communications," Asher added. "They're mobilizing the entire West Coast Security Force. This isn't just another crackdown - they're preparing for something bigger."

Selene produced a holographic display, its green light casting an eerie glow. "Supply chains are being redirected to military installations. They're stockpiling enough resources for a prolonged campaign."

"The plagues have them desperate," Jose said. "Their 'cures' keep failing, and more people are asking questions. They can't maintain control much longer without crushing all resistance."

Enoch moved among the believers, touching each one with his staff. Where the wood met flesh, a brief shimmer passed between them - not a mark or brand, but a blessing that left them standing straighter, eyes clearer.

"We do not fight with weapons of steel or plasma. Leave your rifles here," he said. "Our strength comes from a higher source. Remember what you witnessed in Las Vegas, in New Babylon at the stadium, in the desert? Remember how the Lord provides."

The assembly nodded. They had seen miracles - healing, protection, divine intervention. Their faith wasn't built on ancient stories anymore, but on living testimony of God's power in their midst.

Enoch's staff tapped against the stone floor as he approached the communications hub deep within New Eden's sanctuary. Banks of salvaged monitors cast a blue glow across his weathered features. Jose's team had repurposed abandoned GWC equipment, creating a network that could pierce the government's information blackout.

"The world must witness what comes next," Enoch said. His fingers traced ancient symbols carved into his staff. "Patch into their satellite feeds."

Jose's hands flew across the holographic interface. "We've got access to the major networks. GWC's quantum encryption is good, but their arrogance makes them careless."

Screens flickered to life around them, showing news broadcasts from Seattle to San Diego. The anchors all bore the Mark, their forced smiles never reaching their eyes as they reported on "terrorist activities" by the Commandment Keepers.

"There." Enoch pointed to the largest monitor. "The western seaboard. Center of their power, heart of their false worship."

The staff pulsed with an inner light. Enoch raised it toward the screens, his voice carrying the weight of divine authority. "As Pharaoh's heart was hardened, so to have they closed their eyes to truth. Let darkness fall upon their kingdom."

The monitors crackled with static. In Seattle, a news anchor's eyes widened as the studio lights flickered. San Francisco's feed showed gathering storm clouds that seemed to absorb light itself. Los Angeles disappeared under a rolling wave of unnatural shadow.

"All channels are live," Jose confirmed. "They can't shut this down fast enough. The entire world is watching."

The darkness spread like spilled ink across the western states. Satellites captured its inexorable advance - a supernatural twilight that no emergency lighting could penetrate. Millions of Marked citizens found themselves plunged into a blackness deeper than night, while those who had refused the Mark could still see clearly.

"Let them feel the weight of their chosen blindness," Enoch declared into the broadcasting equipment. His words cut through the GWC's censors, reaching every screen and speaker. "Three days of darkness, that they might know the power of the Most High."

* * *

In the GWC's western command center, Damien Folk paced before the emergency broadcast equipment. Sweat beaded on his forehead despite the climate-controlled environment. The darkness pressed against him like a living thing.

"Our meteorological experts suggest this anomaly results from an unprecedented atmospheric disturbance," he announced, his voice steady despite the tremor in his hands. "Preliminary data indicates unauthorized weather manipulation by extremist elements."

Saul stood at his side, fingers drumming against the polished obsidian desk. The Mark on his hand pulsed with an angry red glow - the only light visible through the impenetrable blackness that surrounded them like living walls.

"The Green World Church assures all citizens that contingency measures are in place," Saul added. "Our quantum generators will restore power and light within hours."

But the backup systems failed. The nuclear plants went dark. Even the military's classified energy reserves couldn't pierce the supernatural shroud.

"Sir," a technician called out, "we're getting reports from unmarked individuals. They claim they can see perfectly fine in the darkness."

Damien's facade cracked. He slammed his fist against the desk. "Suppress those reports. Lock down all independent communications."

"It's too late," Saul muttered. "Social feeds are exploding with testimonies. The unmarked are leading people to safety while our own security forces stumble around blind."

Through the command center's windows, they watched their empire of light and order descend into chaos. Emergency vehicles sat abandoned in the streets. The proud towers of their technological achievement stood as useless monuments in the dark.

"This is no weather anomaly," Saul whispered, touching his Mark as it burned against his skin. "This is-"

"Don't say it," Damien snapped. "We cannot acknowledge any power greater than the Church. The system depends on our authority."

But in the darkness that no human power could dispel, their carefully constructed narrative began to crumble.

For three days, their world remained locked in unnatural darkness. When light finally returned, the GWC's command center buzzed with frantic activity as systems rebooted and communications restored.

Damien Folk stared at the main display screen, his fingers white-knuckled around the edge of his desk. Static crackled across the feed before resolving into a clear signal. A voice, deep and resonant, filled the room.

"This is your final warning. The armies of the GWC must not approach New Eden. All who venture near will be lost."

The transmission cut off. Technicians scrambled to trace its origin, but the signal seemed to come from everywhere and nowhere at once.

Saul's face twisted with rage. "The stranger thinks he can threaten us? We control every satellite in orbit."

"He's gathering followers in New Eden," Damien said. "Intelligence suggests thousands have fled there during the darkness. We can't allow this rebellion to grow."

"Agreed." Saul straightened his uniform and checked his sidearm. "I'll personally lead the assault force. We'll show them what happens to those who defy the Church."

"Take everything we have. Drones, mechanized units, the works. Make an example of them."

Saul nodded and strode toward the door. He paused at the threshold, his Mark pulsing with an angry crimson glow. "What if... what if the darkness wasn't just some technological trick?"

"Don't tell me you're buying into their supernatural nonsense." Damien's voice dripped with contempt. "We are the only true power left in this world. Now go. Crush them."

CHAPTER 19

The sun hung low in the sky, casting long shadows over the desert floor as Enoch trudged through the parched landscape. Dust clung to his cloak, remnants of the journey from the bustling city back to the wilderness where whispers of hope lingered among the Commandment Keepers. He adjusted his hood, obscuring his face from potential watchers.

A rustle drew his attention. A figure stepped from behind a scraggly bush—Jose, with worry etched across his features.

"Enoch!" Jose rushed forward, scanning their surroundings. "Saul's men are prowling close. We can't stay here long."

Enoch nodded, urgency stirring within him. "We need to gather everyone. The GWC's grip tightens by the hour."

Jose glanced back towards their camp, anxiety gnawing at him. "They're ready for a fight. I heard they've armed themselves."

"Good." Enoch's voice held a firm resolve that surprised even him. "Let them come."

As they approached their hidden gathering place—a cluster of weather-beaten tents surrounded by rocky outcroppings—faint voices carried on the wind.

"Keep your heads down," Enoch instructed, slipping into the makeshift meeting area where followers gathered in hushed tones.

Lydia stood near the center, her hands clasped tightly in prayer. She raised her head as Enoch entered, eyes brightening with recognition and hope.

"We were afraid," she confessed softly. "The GWC is spreading fear like wildfire."

"They want to extinguish our flame," Enoch said, heart pounding in his chest. "But fear will not lead us to salvation."

The group murmured their agreement, fists clenching with determination.

"Saul believes he can silence us," Jose added, pacing slightly. "But if we stand united—"

"—We can withstand anything," Lydia interrupted passionately.

A sudden crash echoed outside—the unmistakable sound of heavy boots trampling toward them.

"Get ready!" Enoch's voice cut through the tension as he grasped his rod tightly.

The door flap whipped open as Saul stormed in, flanked by armed guards clad in dark uniforms emblazoned with the GWC insignia.

"Surround them!" Saul commanded, sneering at Enoch. "You think you can rally these lost souls against us? You're mistaken!"

Enoch squared his shoulders and met Saul's glare head-on.

"You underestimate faith," he shot back defiantly. "Your power holds no weight against divine truth."

Saul's lips twisted into a scornful smile as he motioned for his guards to advance.

"Seize him!" he barked.

The atmosphere thickened with anticipation; every heartbeat felt like thunder in Enoch's ears as he raised his rod high above his head.

"I call upon Heaven!" His voice resonated with authority, reverberating through the tense air.

Light erupted around him—a blinding flash that sent Saul's guards stumbling back in shock.

The blinding light subsided, leaving Saul's men disoriented. Through the settling dust, ranks of Commandment Keepers emerged from their hiding places among the rocks and tents. Their numbers swelled—hundreds upon hundreds stepping forward with quiet determination.

A cool breeze swept through the gathering, carrying with it an otherworldly presence that made the air shimmer. The GWC guards shifted uneasily, their weapons suddenly feeling inadequate against this unseen force.

"Kneel," Lydia called out, dropping to her knees. The rest of the Keepers followed suit, creating a rippling wave of movement across the desert floor.

Jose raised his hands skyward. "Holy Father, shield Your faithful servants."

The atmosphere grew thick, charged with an electric intensity that made hair stand on end. Several Remnant began singing and blowing ancient ram horn trumpets, their voices blending into a haunting melody that echoed off the rocky walls.

Enoch felt it first—the unmistakable presence of celestial beings. Though invisible to mortal eyes, their power radiated through the gathering. The Remnant' faces glowed with renewed strength, their fears melting away like morning frost.

"The Host surrounds us," Enoch declared, his voice carrying across the assembly. "Stand firm in your faith."

The Commandment Keepers rose as one, their movements synchronized, as if guided by an unseen hand. They formed circles within circles, each person linking hands with those beside them. Their prayers grew stronger, more confident—a symphony of devotion that seemed to make the very ground beneath them pulse with energy.

Even Saul's men noticed the change. Their earlier bravado crumbled as they witnessed the transformation of what they'd dismissed as a ragtag group of rebels into an army fortified by divine presence.

The air continued to buzz with supernatural energy as the Commandment Keepers prepared themselves, their ritual prayers building to a crescendo. Each person stood taller, shoulders squared, faces set with unwavering resolve. They were ready.

The ground trembled beneath the weight of military vehicles as GWC forces spread across the desert landscape. Tanks rolled forward, their metal tracks grinding against rock and sand. Behind them, rows of soldiers marched in perfect formation, their boots kicking up clouds of dust that hung in the air like a shroud.

Saul and his men ran towards the approaching armour armada, quickly jumping atop a command vehicle, surveying his assembled army through binoculars. Five thousand strong. They formed a sea of green uniforms and polished weapons that stretched to the horizon. The morning sun glinted off rifle barrels and helmet visors.

"Sir, all units report ready," a lieutenant approached, tablet in hand.

Saul lowered his binoculars, a cold smile playing across his features. "Excellent. The Commandment Keepers won't stand a chance against modern warfare."

The air grew heavy, thick with an oppressive presence that made several soldiers shift uncomfortably. Dark shapes flickered at the edge of vision, there and gone in an instant. Whispers carried on the wind, speaking words that bypassed ears and went straight to the mind.

They mock your strength, the voices hissed. *Show them your power.*

A young soldier gripped his rifle tighter, knuckles white. "Did you hear that?"

"Hear what?" his companion snapped, but sweat beaded on his forehead despite the morning chill.

They deserve destruction; the whispers continued. *Their faith makes them weak.*

The ranks began to stir, soldiers glancing over their shoulders at shadows that shouldn't exist. Hatred bubbled up in their hearts, mixed with tendrils of fear they couldn't explain. Some began to shake, while others grew rigid with barely contained rage.

Saul felt it too - an unnatural darkness pressing against his thoughts, feeding his determination with promises of victory and power. He embraced it, letting the whispers fuel his resolve.

"Today," he announced through the command channel, his voice reaching every soldier's earpiece, "we crush this rebellion once and for all."

The army responded with a cheer, but underneath their shouts, the demons' whispers grew louder, more insistent, weaving through the ranks like poison.

The first artillery shells screamed through the morning air. Enoch lifted his staff, its ancient wood warm against his palms. The Commandment Keepers stood shoulder to shoulder, their prayers rising above the approaching thunder of war machines.

"Hold fast," Enoch commanded, his voice carrying across the assembly.

The shells struck—not earth and flesh, but an invisible wall that shimmered with otherworldly light. Each impact burst into brilliant fragments, raining back toward the GWC forces in arcs of divine retribution. Tanks lurched to a halt, their crews bailing out as their own ammunition boomeranged through their ranks.

Saul's jaw clenched as he watched the impossible scene unfold. "Switch to ground assault! Move in!"

But his troops hesitated, their formations breaking as confusion spread. Soldiers pointed skyward where translucent figures towered above the battlefield, their presence both terrible and beautiful. Wings of light stretched across the horizon, creating a dome of protection over the faithful.

"What sorcery is this?" A GWC commander grabbed his radio. "Fall back! Regroup!"

More artillery fire met the same fate, exploding against the celestial barrier and cascading back upon the attackers. Vehicles burst into flames. Soldiers scattered, their weapons useless against the heavenly defense.

Through the chaos, Enoch stood unmoved, his staff glowing with an inner fire. The Commandment Keepers' voices rose in perfect harmony, their faith manifesting as visible waves of power that reinforced the angels' shield.

Saul's army dissolved into disorder. Tank commanders reversed their vehicles, crushing their own people in their haste to retreat. Infantry broke ranks, dropping weapons as they fled from the supernatural display.

"Stand and fight!" Saul screamed into his command mic, but static was his only answer. His modern army, with all its technological might, crumbled before ancient power beyond their understanding.

Dark shapes slithered between the GWC ranks like oil through water. The soldiers' expressions twisted as unseen claws raked across their minds. A young private dropped his rifle, pressing his palms against his temples.

Kill them all, the shadows whispered. *Destroy everything.*

"Get out of my head!" Another soldier collapsed to his knees, tears streaming down his face.

The darkness coalesced into vague humanoid forms—writhing masses of shadow that darted between the troops. Their touch left frost on weapons and armor, spreading a bone-deep chill through the battlefield.

They mock your strength, the demons hissed. *Your comrades plot against you.*

A sergeant turned his gun on his own squad. His hands shook as he fought against the compulsion. "Stay back! You're all traitors!"

The shadows swirled faster, feeding on the growing panic and mistrust. Soldiers fired wildly into empty air, their shots passing harmlessly through the mystic forms. Others huddled behind vehicles, rocking back and forth as the whispers grew louder.

Your leaders have abandoned you, the voices crooned. *There is only death here.*

The disciplined army fractured further. Squad leaders barked contradictory orders. Tanks reversed direction, their crews deaf to commands. The air grew thick with the stench of sulfur and decay.

Saul watched his forces crumble, unaware of the dark figure on his shoulder, whispering sweet corruption into his ear. His eyes blazed with an unnatural light as he grabbed his radio.

"Kill them all!" he screamed, spittle flying from his lips. "I don't care about casualties! Burn everything!"

The shadows rippled with pleasure at his words, their forms growing more substantial as they fed on his rage. They spread through the ranks like a plague, turning soldier against soldier, commander against commander.

The once-mighty army devolved into chaos, their weapons and training useless against an enemy they couldn't fight. The darkness had found its foothold, and it would not easily let go.

The heavens split open with blinding radiance. Waves of celestial beings descended through the rift, their wings trailing streams of golden light. Each angel stood taller than the tanks below, their forms both beautiful and terrifying. The air crackled with divine energy as they engaged the writhing shadows plaguing the GWC forces.

An angel's sword cleaved through a cluster of demons, its light dispersing the darkness like smoke in the wind. The shadows screamed—not with sound, but with a psychic force that made soldiers clutch their heads in agony.

Among the Commandment Keepers, Enoch raised his staff higher. The angels' presence formed a protective dome of light around the faithful, their wings interlocking to create an impenetrable barrier.

Through the chaos, a darker presence emerged. It towered above the other shadows, its form more solid, more real. Blood-red eyes fixed upon Saul as it glided toward him, trailing wisps of darkness like a tattered cloak.

"They fear your strength," it whispered, its voice like steel scraping bone. "You've seen what their faith has done—dividing families, destroying order. But you could restore it all."

Saul's grip on his command console tightened. The demon's words slithered through his mind, awakening doubts he'd buried long ago.

"Remember the truth you once knew," the demon continued, circling him. "Before their God demanded submission. Before, they claimed exclusive rights to salvation. You could unite humanity under one banner—yours."

Sweat beaded on Saul's forehead as memories surfaced—childhood prayers, his mother's gentle teachings about Jesus, moments of pure faith he'd abandoned in pursuit of power. The demon's presence pressed against these memories, trying to twist them into something darker.

"Their God is weak," it hissed. "Look how He hides behind angels while we offer real power. Take it. Command it. Make the world kneel before your vision."

The demon's influence wrapped around Saul like chains of shadow, each link forged from pride, ambition, and forgotten truth.

The sky erupted in a spectacular display of light and shadow as angels clashed with demons above the battlefield. Divine energy crackled through the air, sending shockwaves that knocked GWC soldiers off their feet. Dark tendrils whipped through the ranks, leaving frost and decay in their wake.

An angel's sword sliced through three demons, their essence dissolving into mist. The demons retaliated, launching waves of darkness that the celestial beings deflected with shields of pure light. Each impact sent ripples of energy cascading down to earth, scorching the ground in patterns of light and shadow.

The Commandment Keepers advanced steadily, their prayers creating a barrier that pushed back the darkness. Jose led the front line, his voice rising above the chaos as he quoted ancient scriptures. Lydia flanked him, her hands raised in supplication as she moved forward.

Above his command vehicle, Saul gripped the railing as memories flooded his mind. The demon's presence grew stronger, feeding off his inner turmoil.

"Your mother was wrong," it whispered, its voice like ice in his veins. "All those Sunday mornings, all those bedtime prayers—empty rituals that kept you weak."

Saul's knees buckled. "No... she believed—"

"She believed in fairy tales," the demon cut in, wrapping darker tendrils around his thoughts. "You've built something real. Something powerful. Why throw it away for their God?"

The air around Saul grew thick with shadow, distorting the battlefield before him. His troops scattered in confusion while the Keepers advanced with unwavering purpose. Each step they took seemed to push back the darkness, and something deep within him recognized their power as truth.

"They're winning," he muttered, doubt creeping into his voice.

The demon's form solidified, drawing strength from Saul's uncertainty. "They only appear to win. Stay strong. Stay faithful to your cause."

But Saul's hands trembled as he watched another wave of angels descend, their light piercing through the demon's influence. The truth he'd buried for so long clawed its way to the surface, bringing with it the weight of every choice that had led him here.

Through the chaos of battle, a fierce bark cut across the field. Rollo, the Commandment keeper's German Shepherd form silhouetted against the supernatural light, bounded forward with purposeful strides. His hackles raised, teeth bared, he locked onto Saul and the demon hovering near him.

The demon's form rippled, its attention drawn from Saul to this new threat. Rollo's eyes blazed with an inner fire as he advanced, each step leaving prints of light in the dusty ground.

Saul stumbled back against his command vehicle. "What—"

Rollo launched himself forward, his powerful muscles propelling him through the air. As he leaped, Enoch raised his staff, channeling divine energy toward the faithful hound. Light wrapped around Rollo's form like a mantle, transforming his bark into something that shook the very air.

The sound carried across the battlefield, cutting through the demon's influence. GWC soldiers stopped in their tracks, heads turning toward the source. The dog's presence radiated courage and clarity, breaking through the shadow's hold on their minds.

Rollo landed in front of Saul, his fur crackling with holy energy. Each bark sent pulses of light rippling outward, driving back the darkness that had wrapped itself around the GWC leader. The demon recoiled, its form becoming less substantial with each pulse of divine power flowing through the dog.

Other animals emerged from hiding—birds swooped down from the cliffs, desert foxes darted between the tanks, even a few wild horses appeared on the ridgeline. All moved with purpose, guided by the same light that empowered Rollo, their presence a reminder of a simpler, purer faith.

The demon's grip on Saul weakened as Rollo's divine presence pushed back the darkness. Through the clearing shadows, Saul's eyes met Enoch's across the battlefield. The ancient prophet stepped forward, his staff glowing with celestial fire.

"You remember, don't you?" Enoch's voice carried clearly despite the chaos. "The peace you felt as a child, kneeling beside your bed. Your mother's hand on your shoulder as she taught you about grace."

Saul's legs gave out, and he slumped against his command vehicle. The demon hissed, but its form grew transparent as memories flooded back—pure moments of faith untainted by ambition.

"I wanted to save them," Saul whispered, his voice cracking. "To unite everyone under one banner. How did it become this?"

"By forgetting whose banner truly matters." Enoch closed the distance between them, each step leaving traces of light in the dust. "You traded truth for power, love for control."

The demon lashed out with tendrils of darkness, but they dissipated against Enoch's aura. Rollo stood guard, his supernatural bark keeping the shadow at bay.

"Your mother's prayers follow you still," Enoch continued, his eyes reflecting divine wisdom. "They echo in the chambers of heaven, waiting for your return."

Tears streaked down Saul's face as the weight of his choices crashed over him. Years of justified cruelty, of twisted scripture, of persecution—all of it laid bare before ancient truth.

"What have I done?" Saul's hands shook as he stared at them, seeing blood where none existed. "How many have I hurt? How many have I led astray?"

The demon's voice grew desperate, but its words no longer found purchase in Saul's mind. Before him stood a man who had walked with God, whose every word rang with authority that no earthly power could match.

Enoch lifted his staff toward the heavens, his voice carrying ancient power. "Let Your light shine forth!"

The angels responded with a coordinated movement that rippled across the sky. Their wings spread wide, creating a cascading wave of pure radiance that descended upon the battlefield. The light penetrated every shadow, every crevice, leaving nowhere for darkness to hide.

Demons shrieked as the divine energy tore through their ranks. Their shadowy forms dissolved like smoke in a strong wind, leaving behind only echoes of their corrupting whispers. The ground trembled beneath the clash of spiritual forces, creating patterns of light that spread like cracks through the earth.

GWC soldiers dropped to their knees as the wave of holy energy washed over them. Some wept openly as years of indoctrination crumbled under the weight of undeniable truth. Others stood frozen, their weapons forgotten as they witnessed power beyond their comprehension.

"The plagues!" A soldier pointed at his arm where sores began forming beneath his uniform. "It's happening again!"

The affliction spread rapidly through the GWC ranks. Those who bore the Mark of the Green World Church clutched their heads and bodies as divine judgment manifested in physical form. Their carefully constructed defenses against the first plague dissolved under this new assault.

Demons fled in chaos, their forms shredding apart in the intense light. Each angelic pulse drove them further back, their influence over the soldiers weakening with each retreat. The air cleared of their corrupting presence, leaving behind an almost painful clarity.

Through the purifying light, the Commandment Keepers advanced. Their prayers rose stronger now, harmonizing with the angels' presence. Where their feet touched the ground, the earth itself seemed to respond, trembling in recognition of divine authority.

The combined force of spiritual and physical plagues staggered the GWC forces. Soldiers struggled to maintain formation as both fear and conviction gripped their hearts. Some threw down their weapons, falling to their knees in surrender, while others backed away, their training useless against powers beyond mortal understanding.

The remaining GWC soldiers wavered, their weapons hanging loose in trembling hands. One by one, rifles clattered to the ground. A young private stepped forward, tears cutting clean tracks through the dust on his face.

"I remember my grandmother's Bible," he said. "The stories she read to me as a child."

Others followed, drawn toward the light that emanated from Enoch and the Commandment Keepers. The angels' presence pressed against them, not with force but with a gentle conviction that broke through years of indoctrination.

Saul gripped the railing of his command vehicle, his knuckles white. The demon's whispers grew fainter, but still pulled at the edges of his consciousness. His life's work crumbled around him—the carefully built empire of control and false unity dissolving under divine truth.

"Your choice remains your own," Enoch said, extending his hand toward Saul. "As it has always been."

The staff in Enoch's other hand pulsed with celestial fire. Rollo stood guard, his supernatural presence a barrier between Saul and the retreating darkness. The demon's form flickered like a candle in the wind, its influence weakening with each soldier who stepped into the light.

Across the battlefield, Jose and the Commandment Keepers moved among the fallen, offering water and comfort to those afflicted by the plague. Some GWC soldiers still clutched their weapons, faces twisted with uncertainty as they watched their comrades choose sides.

The angels maintained their defensive formation, wings spread wide to shield the growing group of converts. Their light cast long shadows across the scarred earth, where patches of scorched ground marked the demons' retreat.

Saul dismounted his vehicle took a halting step forward, then stopped. His fingers brushed the GWC insignia on his uniform—the symbol of everything he'd built, everything he'd believed would save humanity. The choice before him stretched like a chasm, with no middle ground to stand upon.

CHAPTER 20

Enoch's staff glowed with divine light as he faced Saul across the scarred battlefield. The defeated GWC commander's shoulders slumped, his uniform stained with dust and sweat. Around them, angels maintained their protective circle while demons lurked at the edges of perception, waiting.

"Satan owns the fence on indecision," Enoch's words cut through the tense silence. "Your heart knows the difference between truth and lies."

Saul's hand trembled as he touched the GWC insignia on his chest. The Mark beneath his uniform burned, a physical reminder of his allegiance to the false church. His eyes darted between the retreating darkness and the pure light emanating from Enoch's staff.

"Everything I built..." Saul's voice cracked. "Everything I believed would unite humanity."

"Built on shifting sand," Enoch stepped closer. "Your foundation was pride, not truth."

The remaining GWC soldiers watched their leader, their own choices hanging in balance. Some had already crossed to stand with the Commandment Keepers, while others clustered in uncertain groups, weapons lowered but not discarded.

Rollo padded forward, his supernatural presence pushing back the lingering shadows around Saul. The dog's eyes held ancient wisdom as he stood between the two men, tail straight and alert.

Angels' wings stirred the air, creating ripples of light that exposed every shadow. No darkness could hide from the divine radiance that now filled the battlefield. The demons' whispers grew fainter, their influence breaking against the wall of celestial power.

Enoch stood firm, his victory clear in the transformed landscape around them. Where chaos and violence had reigned moments before, peace settled like morning dew. The authority of heaven flowed through him, undeniable and absolute.

Saul's fingers traced the GWC Mark beneath his uniform. "We meant to save the planet, to unite humanity under one banner."

"The created became your god." Enoch's staff pulsed with divine light. "Earth groans under humankind's attempts to control what was freely given. Your laws chain people to fear while claiming to protect them."

The remaining GWC soldiers shifted, their weapons hanging loose. The Mark burned on each of their bodies as truth pierced through generations of deception.

"His commandments were written in stone," Enoch continued, "not in shifting regulations that change with each council meeting. The Sabbath was His gift, His Mark not a burden to be replaced by convenience."

Rollo's ears perked up as angels drew closer, their presence intensifying the holy atmosphere. The dog's supernatural awareness detected the last traces of demonic influence retreating from Saul's mind.

"The cross..." Saul's voice broke. "We replaced it with an empty ritual."

"His blood paid the price once and for all." Enoch stepped forward. "No human sacrifice of comfort or freedom can match what was finished on Calvary. Those who accept this gift find true liberty - not in following man's rules, but in walking His path."

The Mark on Saul's right hand flared with pain, a physical manifestation of the spiritual battle raging within. The choice crystallized before him: continue serving the system he'd helped build, or embrace the freedom purchased at such a terrible price two thousand years ago.

A blinding light burst from Enoch's staff, knocking Saul to his knees. The GWC commander pressed his palms against his eyes as divine radiance seared through him, stripping away layers of pride and deception.

"Saul! Saul! Why do you persecute me?" The voice thundered across the battlefield, yet seemed to speak directly into his soul.

"Who... who are you?" Saul's body trembled.

"I am Yahshua, whom you persecute when you hunt my faithful ones."

The Mark on Saul's right hand burned like molten metal. He clawed at his uniform, desperate to tear away the symbol that now felt like poison against his skin. His fingers found only scarred flesh where the Mark had been.

"Lord..." Saul's voice broke. "What would you have me do?"

The light receded, leaving Saul blinking at the dirt. His eyes could no longer focus - the world had become a blur of shadows and light. But his spiritual sight had never been clearer. Every lie he'd believed, every false doctrine he'd enforced, every innocent believer he'd persecuted - the weight of it crushed him.

Rollo approached, pressing his warm fur against Saul's side. The dog's presence anchored him as waves of divine truth washed through his mind. Enoch knelt beside him, placing a gentle hand on his shoulder.

"Brother," Enoch said, "the scales have fallen from your eyes. Rise and be baptized, washing away your sins."

Tears streamed down Saul's face as decades of false teaching crumbled away, replaced by pure truth. The same passion that had driven him to persecute the faithful now burned with the desire to proclaim the gospel he'd once tried to destroy.

The divine light receded, leaving the battlefield bathed in an ethereal glow. Saul's transformation rippled through the ranks of GWC soldiers. Several dropped to their knees, tears streaming down faces that had moments ago been twisted with hatred.

"The Mark - it burns!" A young soldier clutched his forehead, stumbling forward. Others caught him, their own expressions shifting from confusion to recognition as the truth penetrated their hearts.

"Brothers, sisters," Enoch raised his staff. "The Creator calls you to freedom."

A group of thirty soldiers moved forward, dropping their weapons. The Marks on their bodies faded as they approached, leaving only smooth skin behind. Their uniforms, once symbols of oppression, hung loose like shed snake skins.

"We were blind," one woman whispered, touching her unmarked hand in wonder.

But not all hearts softened to the divine call. Captain Reynolds backed away, clutching his rifle. His face contorted as he fought against conviction. Two dozen soldiers followed his lead, forming a tight defensive cluster.

"This is heresy," Reynolds spat. "The Church protects order. Without it, chaos reigns." He signaled a retreat, and his loyal soldiers melted into the shadows beyond the angels' light.

Rollo watched them go, his ears flat against his head. The dog's supernatural senses detected the demons following the retreating soldiers, wrapping them in darker shadows of deception.

The converted soldiers gathered around Saul and Enoch, their faces glowing with newfound purpose. Where the Mark of the GWC had been, divine light now shone from within. The angels drew closer, their presence strengthening this pocket of truth in a world still gripped by lies.

Saul knelt in the dirt, his unseeing eyes turned inward as memories washed over him. The physical blindness forced him to see with his heart - every moment of persecution, every faithful believer he'd condemned, every false doctrine he'd defended as truth.

"I was so certain," he whispered, his voice rough with emotion. "The Green World Church promised unity, promised salvation through human effort. But it was all pride."

Enoch's steady presence beside him anchored Saul as the divine truth continued, restructuring his understanding. The passion that had driven him to hunt down Commandment Keepers now burned with holy fire.

"Three days ago, I ordered the death of believers." His hands trembled. "I thought I served righteousness. Instead, I fought against the very God I claimed to represent."

Rollo pressed closer, the dog's supernatural warmth cutting through the chill of conviction. Saul's fingers found the German Shepherd's fur, drawing comfort from the creature's unwavering faith.

"The Mark..." Saul touched his right hand where the GWC symbol had burned. "It blinded us to truth. Every regulation, every new law - we replaced God's perfect commandments with human tradition. We traded freedom for control."

Divine light pulsed through him, washing away decades of deception. Where rigid doctrine had ruled, grace now flowed. Where fear had driven his actions, love took root. The transformation pierced deeper than mere belief - it reshaped his very identity.

"I persecuted the faithful," Saul's voice broke. "Now I see through fresh eyes, though these physical ones are dark. His power is made perfect in weakness."

Divine light pulsed from Enoch's staff as he placed his hand on Saul's shoulder. The former GWC commander remained on his knees, head bowed in reverence.

"The Lord has chosen you for His purpose," Enoch's voice carried across the battlefield. "As He transformed Saul of Tarsus, so He transforms you. From this day forward, you shall be called Paul - a vessel of His grace."

Paul lifted his sightless eyes, tears streaming down his face. The new name settled over him like a mantle of purpose, washing away the last vestiges of his former identity.

Rollo padded forward at Enoch's gesture. The German Shepherd's supernatural presence radiated strength and protection as he sat beside Paul.

"Rollo will guard and guide you," Enoch said. "His sight will be yours until the Lord restores your vision. His faithfulness will remind you of the path ahead."

Paul's hand found Rollo's fur, feeling the divine connection between them. The dog pressed closer, accepting his new mission with quiet dignity.

Enoch turned to the converted soldiers who stood watching, their faces still glowing with newfound faith. Their GWC uniforms hung loose, like empty shells of their former lives.

"Welcome, brothers and sisters, to the remnant church," Enoch spread his arms wide. "You join a lineage of faithful ones who have kept His commandments through all generations. Here you will find truth, not tradition. Freedom, not fear."

The converts advanced together, following the radiant light of acceptance. Where the Mark of the Beast had once caused pain, peace now prevailed. Their eyes gleamed with determination as they surrounded their newfound faith community. Enoch signals for Jose to step forward. "Jose will lead you all to New Eden," Enoch looks at Jose with eyes of compassion. "I must depart. I have a separate journey that I must travel alone. You are now the shepherd of the Remnant church. Lead, teach, and nurture them."

***

Captain Reynolds burst through the polished doors of New Babylon GWC headquarters, his uniform caked with dirt and blood. The pristine marble floors squeaked under his boots as he rushed toward Damien Folk's office.

The guards parted at his approach, recognizing the wild desperation in his eyes. Without waiting for clearance, Reynolds shoved open the heavy oak door.

Damien Folk looked up from his desk. His fingers paused over a holographic display. "This better be important, Captain."

"Sir, Saul..." Reynolds steadied himself against a chair. "He's turned against us. The entire west coast army - we lost them all to that prophet's lies."

Folk's face hardened. His hand crushed the report he'd been holding. "Explain."

"Light everywhere. Angels, sir. Real ones." Reynolds wiped sweat from his brow. "Saul fell to his knees. Started spouting scripture. His

Mark - it vanished. Others followed. Three hundred of our best men, gone."

Folk stood, his tall frame casting a shadow across the room. "Saul was our strongest commander. His loyalty was absolute."

"He goes by Paul now. Claims divine revelation." Reynolds swallowed hard. "The prophet... he has power we can't match."

"No one is beyond our reach." Folk's voice cut like steel. "Issue an arrest warrant for Saul - maximum security protocols. Dead or alive."

He turned to the window, staring out at New Babylon's gleaming towers. "This defeat cannot stand. Prepare my transport to Las Vegas headquarters. We'll regroup, strengthen our position."

"Sir, what about-"

"That's all, Captain." Folk's dismissal brooked no argument. "Ensure the warrant goes out immediately. I want Saul in chains by nightfall."

Reynolds saluted and backed out of the office, leaving Folk alone with his darkening thoughts.

***

Damien Folk strode down the steel-lined corridor of GWC's New Babylon complex, his footsteps echoing against the walls. Two armed guards flanked him, their weapons charged and ready.

"The guard on his left said, 'I prepped the interrogation room.'"

Folk nodded. The holding cells came into view - a row of reinforced glass chambers filled with captured Commandment Keepers. Their faces pressed against the barriers, eyes burning with defiance despite days of questioning.

A woman in a white lab coat approached, tablet in hand. "Sir, we've analyzed the latest data from the Mark recipients. The sores are spreading faster than our treatments can contain them."

"Double the dosage." Folk's jaw clenched. "And get me everything we have on Saul's last known location."

"Paul, sir. He's going by Paul now."

"I don't care what he calls himself." Folk stopped at the security terminal, pressing his palm against the scanner. "He's a traitor who needs to be dealt with."

The door slid open with a hydraulic hiss. Inside, screens covered the walls, displaying surveillance feeds from across the west coast. Analysts hunched over keyboards, tracking movement patterns and scanning facial recognition hits.

"Sir." A technician waved him over. "We picked up unusual energy signatures near the old church district in Las Vegas. Similar readings to what we recorded during the prophet's appearances."

Folk leaned closer to the display. The thermal imaging revealed a cluster of heat signatures gathered in what appeared to be an abandoned warehouse. "How many?"

"At least fifty. Could be more inside where our sensors can't penetrate."

"Send in a strike team. Full tactical gear." Folk straightened. "I want them brought in alive if possible. Dead if necessary."

The technician's fingers flew across the keys, relaying the orders. Folk watched the red dots of the strike team converge on the location, his reflection grim in the darkened screen.

CHAPTER 21

Thunder rolled across the Las Vegas sky, transforming the neon-lit strip into an eerie twilight. The GWC strike team moved in formation toward the warehouse, their boots silent against the cracked pavement. Team Leader Linn Fo Chen signaled his squad to take position around the perimeter.

The warehouse loomed before them, its weathered walls decorated with faded murals of saints. Light leaked through the gaps in the boarded windows, accompanied by the soft murmur of voices raised in prayer.

"Alpha team in position." Chen's radio crackled."Heat signatures confirm twenty-plus targets inside."

"Copy that." Chen adjusted his tactical gear."Breach on my Mark-"

The sky split open. A bolt of lightning struck the ground between the strike team and the warehouse entrance, leaving a smoking crater in the concrete. The air grew thick, heavy with the scent of ozone.

Inside the warehouse, Enoch raised his head from prayer. The wooden staff in his hands hummed with energy, its surface glowing with an inner light. Around him, the faithful continued their worship, undisturbed by the gathering storm.

"Proceed with caution," Chen ordered, his voice steady despite the supernatural display. "Gas protocols authorized-"

Another thunderclap shook the building's foundation. The sky darkened to an unnatural purple, clouds swirling in a vortex above the warehouse. Wind whipped through the alley, scattering debris and forcing the strike team to brace against walls and vehicles.

"Sir," a soldier called out, pointing upward."Look!"

Through gaps in the churning clouds, glimpses of brilliant light pulsed. The strike team's equipment sparked and fizzled, radio communications dissolving into static.

Chen stared at the warehouse door, his finger tight on his weapon's trigger. The heavens groaned again, a sound that vibrated through his bones and set his teeth on edge. His Mark burned beneath his uniform, a searing reminder of his allegiance to the GWC.

The first hailstone crashed through the roof of the Bellagio like a meteor, crushing three floors before embedding itself in the casino's marble foundation. Each frozen projectile measured larger than a VW Beetle, their crystalline surfaces refracting the city's neon glow as they plummeted from the purple-black sky.

The city erupted, screams filled the Strip as tourists and locals alike fled for shelter. A massive hailstone obliterated the replica Eiffel Tower, sending steel girders and concrete raining down on the panicked crowds below. The hail crushed cars like tin cans, their alarms wailing in a cacophony of destruction.

Alarms and alerts blared in the New Babylon command room, monitors showing the destructive storm leaving Las Vegas in ruins. The Luxor's beam flickered and died. The Mirage disappeared in a cloud of debris and frozen shrapnel.

Damien leaned in, eyes fixed on the monitor. His domain crumbled before him. Blocks disappeared as the barrage continued. The desert trembled, forming permanent craters that marred the landscape.

Damien turned to his science minister."This is something else, something we are not prepared for." the minister nodded, but couldn't look away from the destruction.

"Please arrange for a helicopter. We must inform New York. We're headed to the UN headquarters."

As Damien Folk boarded the helicopter, as the aircraft gained altitude, he could see the scorched desert and the battleground where his army lie in defeat. Ahead, the dark purple cloud that rained destruction on the city of sin.

The helicopter stayed clear of the storm. Folk listened to the Emergency frequencies as they crackled with reports of casualties mounting by the minute - fifty thousand souls caught in heaven's fury. Las Vegas, the jewel of the desert, reduced to rubble beneath a biblical deluge of ice.

The warehouse door creaked open. Enoch stepped into the devastated street, his staff casting a soft glow across the rubble. Behind him, twenty-three believers huddled together, their faces a mix of awe and fear at the destruction surrounding their untouched sanctuary.

Ice boulders dotted the landscape like alien monuments, steam rising from their surfaces in the desert heat. The warehouse stood alone amid the wreckage, not a single scratch on its weathered walls.

Enoch turned to face the survivors. His hood fell back, revealing eyes that held both compassion and steel. "Your faith has preserved you through this trial. But greater challenges lie ahead."

He raised his staff toward the eastern horizon. A pillar of cloud materialized, its form distinct against the clearing sky. The column stretched from earth to heaven, moving with purpose across the desert.

"There lies your path to New Eden. Follow the pillar as our ancestors did. It will guide you to safety, to others who keep God's commandments."

An elderly woman stepped forward, her silver hair glinting in the staff's light. "But what about you, Enoch?"

"My journey takes a different road. Your task is to reach the sanctuary, to join with those who remain faithful."

The pillar pulsed with inner light, beckoning. The survivors gathered what few possessions they had, helping the weak and elderly prepare for the journey ahead.

"Remember," Enoch's voice carried across the ruined street. "The Mark of the Beast brings destruction. But the seal of God brings life. Keep His commandments. Trust in His guidance."

The group moved out, following the cloud's path through the devastation. Their forms grew smaller against the vast desert, twenty-three souls walking into exile, into hope.

Enoch watched until the last of the faithful disappeared into the desert haze. The staff in his hands pulsed with renewed energy, casting shadows that danced across the ruined streets of Las Vegas.

A gentle breeze stirred his cloak, carrying the scent of ice and destruction. Zophiel materialized beside him, wings folded against his back, their crystalline surface reflecting the morning light.

"The time has come for a different approach," Zophiel said, extending his hand. In it lay a new cloak, darker than midnight, its fabric seeming to absorb the light around it. "Your role changes with the hearts of men."

Enoch set aside his old garment and donned the new one. The hood settled over his features, leaving only his eyes visible - eyes that had witnessed both heaven's glory and earth's corruption.

"The Green World Church grows stronger," Zophiel continued. "They twist scripture to serve their purposes. The faithful few need more than just miracles now."

"They need truth," Enoch said, his voice carrying the weight of divine wisdom. "Pure, unaltered truth."

The angel nodded, his form beginning to fade. "Remember what you learned in the presence of the Most High. Let His light shine through you, Lampstand."

Enoch gripped his staff tighter, feeling the power flow through it and into him. The name resonated in his spirit - Lampstand. Not just a bearer of light, but a fixed point of illumination in a darkening world.

He turned away from the destruction, his new cloak swirling around him. The path ahead led through shadow, through places where the Green World Church's influence had twisted faith into a tool of control. But where darkness deepened, light shone brighter.

* * *

The elevator hummed as it ascended to the gleaming tower of the UN headquarters. Damien Folk straightened his tie. His reflection fractured across the polished metal walls. The events in Las Vegas and New Eden had shaken the GWC's foundation, but this meeting promised to restore order.

The doors opened to the penthouse suite. No secretary, no security - just a single figure standing at the floor-to-ceiling windows, gazing out over Manhattan.

"Mr. Folk." Silas Ashcroft didn't turn around. His voice carried a melodic quality that seemed to bypass the ears and speak directly to the soul. "Your predecessor's death was... unfortunate."

Damien swallowed hard. "Helena's loss has destabilized our West Coast operations."

"And yet, here you stand." Silas turned, his features perfect in their symmetry, his eyes holding depths that made Damien want to look away. "Ready to shepherd your flock through these troubled times."

Silas gestured to a leather chair. A manila folder lay on the desk between them, marked only with the numbers 5202.

"The faithful require a stronger hand," Silas said, sliding the folder toward Damien. "Project 5202 will provide that guidance."

Damien opened the folder. His eyes widened as he read, color draining from his face.

"This is..." He looked up at Silas, who smiled with infinite patience.

"The next phase. Implementation begins immediately." Silas raised a finger to his lips. "But my involvement remains our secret. The world isn't ready for my emergence. Not yet."

Damien nodded, clutching the folder. "I understand. The GWC will follow your direction without question."

"Good." Silas turned back to the window. "You may go."

The elevator ride down felt longer than the ascent. Damien's hands trembled as he held the folder containing Project 5202. The document would reshape the world - but its true author would remain hidden, pulling strings from shadows.

CHAPTER 22

The sun dipped below the horizon, casting long shadows across New Eden's central courtyard. Hundreds of believers gathered around Jose, their faces illuminated by scattered torches and the fading daylight. The recent converts from Las Vegas huddled close, still bearing the haunted looks of their narrow escape.

Jose raised his hands, silencing the murmurs that rippled through the crowd. "Brothers and sisters, the time has come. Our mission changes today." His voice carried across the gathering, strong and clear. "The prophecies speak of a remnant, those who keep God's commandments and hold fast to their faith. They're out there, scattered and afraid, seeking refuge from the GWC's persecution."

A cool breeze rustled through the crowd, carrying the scent of desert sage.

"We can no longer wait for them to find us," Jose continued, his eyes scanning the faces before him. "The Lord commands us to 'Go Therefore' - to seek these faithful souls and bring them to safety."

"But the GWC patrols-" someone called out.

"The same God who protected us from the plagues will shield us on this mission." Jose pulled out a worn map, holding it up. "We've identified communities across the region where believers still gather in secret. They need our help, our guidance, and most importantly, they need to know they're not alone."

The crowd pressed closer as Jose spread the map across a wooden table. Red marks dotted the parchment, each representing a potential sanctuary of faith.

"We'll move in small groups," Jose traced paths between the markers. "Using the old mining, logging roads and forgotten trails. The GWC controls the main roads, but they can't watch every path through God's creation."

A determined energy spread through the gathering. Hands raised, volunteers already stepping forward to accept the challenge.

"Remember," Jose's voice softened, "we're not just offering physical sanctuary. We're gathering the remnant, preserving the truth in these last days. Each soul we bring to New Eden is another light in the darkness."

Jose rolled up the map and tucked it into his leather satchel. The crowd dispersed into smaller groups, their whispered conversations filling the courtyard with a low hum of purpose. He watched as families embraced, knowing some would leave and not return from their sacred mission.

A young woman approached him, her GWC identification card dangling from a chain around her neck. "I can help identify safe routes through the city sectors. I worked as a transit coordinator before-" She touched the cross pendant nestled beside the ID card. "Before I found the truth."

"Thank you, Sarah." Jose nodded, recognizing her from the Paradise City converts. "Your knowledge could save lives."

The sound of boots on gravel drew their attention. Two men emerged from the shadows, their clothes dusty from travel. "Brother Jose," the taller one called out. "News from the eastern settlements."

Jose motioned them closer, noting their exhausted faces. The shorter man pulled a crumpled paper from his jacket. "The GWC's implementing new checkpoints. They're using some kind of enhanced scanning technology. Detecting unauthorized movement is getting harder."

"The Lord provides a way," Jose said, unfolding the paper. His eyes scanned the hastily drawn diagrams of patrol routes and checkpoint locations. "We'll adapt. Perhaps use the old sewage tunnels, or-"

"There's more," the taller man interrupted."They're offering rewards now. Big ones. For information leading to any gathering places of the faithful."

Jose's jaw tightened. He'd seen this before - neighbor turning against neighbor, fear corrupting community bonds. "Then we move faster. Tonight. The longer we wait, the more souls we risk losing."

He turned back to the scattered groups still lingering in the courtyard. These people had already sacrificed everything for their faith. Now they would risk even more to help others find the same freedom. The weight of their trust pressed against his shoulders like a physical burden.

But as he watched them prepare - checking supplies, sharing knowledge, strengthening each other with prayers and embraces - Jose felt a surge of hope. This was how the early church had survived persecution. This was how God's truth would endure.

Jose watched the last groups disappear into the shadows of New Eden's winding paths. The sound of their footsteps faded, replaced by the gentle whisper of desert wind through the courtyard's weathered pillars. He pulled a folded piece of paper from his pocket, studying the careful script before lifting his gaze.

"Paul," he called out to a figure lingering near the eastern archway. "A moment."

Paul stepped into the torchlight. His face bore the marks of recent transformation - the haunted eyes of one who had glimpsed truth after years of deception. The former GWC leader shoulders tensed as he approached.

"Brother Jose." Paul's voice cracked on the word 'brother,' still unused to this new form of address.

Jose spread the paper on the wooden table. "Your knowledge of GWC protocols could save many lives. These safe houses- at sector seven grid coordinate intersect twelve. Are they still secure?"

"I believe that one's compromised. They installed a new surveillance last week. And sector 13-near the fire station. The local enforcer unit changed their patrol pattern." Paul said as he looked through blind eyes

"Can you help our teams navigate around them?"

"I can do better." Paul straightened, squaring his shoulders. "I know the blind spots in their system. The gaps in their coverage. Let me go with one of the rescue groups."

Jose studied the man's face, searching for any trace of his former identity as Saul, the ruthless GWC commander. He found only earnest determination.

"The same people you once hunted would be with you," Jose said softly.

"Which is why I must go." Paul's hands clenched at his sides. "I know their methods because I helped design them. Every life I save now might balance one I put at risk or taken before."

Jose nodded, reaching into his satchel and pulling out a worn leather harness. He motioned for Rollo to come and sit.

"I've fashioned a harness to fit Rollo. With it, Rollo can be your eyes and guide you on your journey.

"My journey?" Paul asked surprisingly.

"Your zeal is admirable, Paul, but your face is too well-known here. The GWC's reach may be vast, but their memory grows weaker with distance." Jose tapped the Midwest region. "I want you to head east through the mountains, to where the great plains stretch beneath endless sky. You'll find souls thirsting for truth."

Paul's shoulders slumped, but understanding flickered across his features. At his feet, Rollo pressed against his leg, tail swaying gently.

"The dog goes with you," Jose said, scratching behind Rollo's ears. " He not just your eyes, but he has a gift for sensing danger, and more importantly, for sensing truth in people's hearts. You'll need that where you're going."

"But surely he'd be more useful here, with the rescue teams–"

"Rollo chose you, Paul. Since your conversion, he hasn't left your side. That's no coincidence."

Paul felt for the German Shepherd, running his hand through the thick fur. Rollo's intelligent eyes met his, seeming to convey a depth of understanding that transcended words.

"The Midwest communities are scattered, isolated," Jose continued. "Many have rejected the GWC's influence but lack direction, purpose. They need someone who understands both sides of this struggle. Someone who can speak truth from experience."

"Like Paul of Tarsus," Paul whispered, the parallel of his own journey suddenly clear. "From persecutor to preacher."

"Exactly." Jose rolled up the atlas and pressed it into Paul's hands. "Take the old mountain routes. We have friends who will guide you past the checkpoints. Once you're east of the Rockies, you'll find the GWC's grip isn't quite as strong."

Paul and Jose knelt in the flickering torchlight, their heads bowed in prayer. The desert wind whispered through the courtyard, carrying the scent of sage and dust.

"Lord, guide our paths as we separate to serve Your purpose," Jose's voice resonated with quiet strength. "Shield Your servants from those who would silence Your truth."

"Grant us wisdom and courage," Paul added, his words carrying the weight of his transformation. "Let us be worthy of this calling."

As they rose, Paul's blank gaze swept the empty courtyard. "What of Enoch? His presence gave hope to so many."

Jose leaned against the wooden table, his weathered fingers tracing the map's edges. "The Lampstand walks a different path now. The Holy Spirit revealed to me that he faces the final confrontation prophesied in Scripture."

"The anti-christ?" Paul's voice dropped to a whisper.

"Yes. While we gather the remnant, Enoch must confront the great deceiver himself. The one who will emerge from the GWC's inner circle, promising peace but bringing destruction."

"Then the prophecies are reaching their culmination."

Jose nodded, his expression grave. "The signs are clear. The plagues, the persecution, the Mark - all as foretold. Now comes the final deception, when one will arise claiming to be the messiah returned."

"And Enoch stands against this false christ alone?"

"Not alone." Jose's eyes lifted to the star-filled sky. "Never alone. The same power that transformed you from persecutor to preacher walks with him. The same Spirit that guided him from the beginning prepares him for this confrontation."

CHAPTER 23

In the depths of the GWC's UN headquarters, Damien Folk paced across polished marble floors. The setting sun cast long shadows through floor-to-ceiling windows, painting the room in shades of blood red.

A figure materialized from the shadows - tall, elegant, with features that seemed to shift and change depending on the angle of light. His presence filled the room with an otherworldly chill.

"The time has come," the figure said, his voice smooth as silk yet carrying undertones that made Damien's skin crawl. "Project 5205 will cement our control."

Damien spread documents across his mahogany desk. "The infrastructure is ready. We've embedded our people in every major institution."

"Excellent." The figure traced a finger across the papers. Where he touched, the ink seemed to writhe. "The world cries out for a savior. They'll embrace me as their messiah, never suspecting the truth."

"What about the resistance? The Commandment Keepers-"

"Are irrelevant." The figure's eyes flashed with an inner fire. "Once I reveal myself, performing miracles that will astound the masses, even the most devout will question their faith."

Damien nodded, pulling up digital displays showing global networks. "We control the narrative. Every screen, every feed will broadcast your arrival. The GWC's influence reaches into every home."

"Perfect." The figure moved to the window, gazing out at the city below. "Humanity's desperation makes them susceptible. They'll accept any solution, any leader who promises peace."

"And those who resist?"

"Will face the full force of Project 5205." The figure turned, his face momentarily revealing its true nature - something ancient and terrible. "No more half measures. No more tolerance for dissent. The time for subtle manipulation is over."

The United Nations General Assembly chamber hummed with tension. Two hundred world leaders shifted in their seats, their whispers echoing off the marble walls. Armed guards lined the perimeter, their faces masks of stone.

Damien Folk strode to the podium, his footsteps sharp against the floor. The room fell silent.

"Distinguished colleagues, we face unprecedented challenges. Climate disasters. Food shortages. Civil unrest and these terrorist called the lampstand. He gripped the edges of the podium. "But I bring you a solution."

Screens descended from the ceiling, displaying complex diagrams and statistics. "Project 5202 - a comprehensive system of resource management and population control. Through advanced surveillance and biometric tracking, we can ensure equitable distribution of resources."

The French delegate raised his hand. "This level of monitoring - it violates basic human rights."

"Rights mean nothing if humanity destroys itself."Damien's voice cut through the murmurs. "The Green World Church has developed technology to implement this system seamlessly. Every citizen will receive benefits based on their compliance and contribution to society."

The Chinese representative nodded. "How quickly can this be implemented?"

"Within months. Our infrastructure is ready."Damien pulled up new slides showing integration plans. "We need only your vote to proceed."

The Russian delegate leaned forward. "And those who resist?"

"Will lose access to essential services until they comply. The system is designed to encourage voluntary participation."

Debate erupted across the chamber. Damien watched as alliances formed and broke, just as Silas had predicted. After three hours of heated discussion, the vote was called.

The electronic board lit up: 180 in favor, 20 against.

Damien suppressed a smile. "Project 5202 will commence immediately. Your cooperation ensures humanity's survival." He gathered his papers, Silas's words echoing in his mind - keep my identity secret. Let them think this was purely a human solution to human problems.

CHAPTER 24

The sea breeze whipped around Enoch as he materialized on a rocky outcrop overlooking the Aegean Sea. Ancient stone walls and ruins dotted the landscape of Patmos, weathered by centuries of sun and salt air. The island held an otherworldly quality, suspended between past and present.

Zophiel appeared beside him, wings folding into invisibility. "This place holds special significance. Here, John received his revelation of end times."

Enoch ran his hand along the rough stone of a nearby wall. Memories that weren't his own flickered through his mind - visions of a much younger island, of an aged apostle writing furiously by lamplight.

"Your brother Elijah continues his work in America's eastern cities," Zophiel said.

"The Anti-Christ grows bold," Enoch said. "I feel his darkness spreading."

"Yes. Soon he will reveal himself to the world." Zophiel's form shimmered in the Mediterranean sun. "When that day comes, you and Elijah must stand together as the two olive trees prophesied. Your combined light will pierce his deception."

The angel gestured toward an ancient cave carved into the hillside. "Wait there. Prepare yourself. The final confrontation approaches, but you must not face it alone. Unity between the Lampstands is essential."

Enoch gazed across the sparkling waters, sensing the weight of prophecy settling around him. The cave beckoned - the same one where John had received his apocalyptic visions. History and destiny intertwined on this sacred isle.

Enoch's gaze remained fixed on the horizon, his thoughts drifting back to those he'd left behind. The weight of their absence pressed against his chest.

"What of Jose and Paul? The remnant who stood faithful through the persecution?"

Zophiel stepped closer, wings rustling in the sea breeze. "Jose leads them well. The faithful gather in mountain caves, sharing what little food remains. Their numbers grow daily as more flee the GWC's control."

"And Paul?" Enoch's voice softened at the mention of his former adversary.

"His transformation mirrors his namesake. Like Saul of Tarsus, he now preaches with the same passion he once used to persecute. The GWC hunts him, but he moves between communities, strengthening the believers."

Enoch traced the weathered grooves on his staff. "They face such danger."

"The Holy Spirit protects them. Jose's radio broadcasts reach even the most remote areas, guiding seekers to safety. Paul's testimony shakes the very foundation of the GWC's power structure. Many of his former colleagues now question their allegiance."

"Will they survive what's coming?"

"Their path is their own to walk," Zophiel said. "Just as you must walk yours. The remnant's strength lies not in numbers, but in their unshakeable faith. They understand the cost of their choice."

Enoch sank down onto a sun-warmed rock, his shoulders dropping with exhaustion. The endless waves crashed against Patmos' shore below, their rhythm matching the weariness in his bones. His fingers traced the worn grooves of his staff, memories washing over him like the tide.

"I'm tired, my old friend." His voice carried the weight of countless battles. "I long for the days of peace and tranquility. My walk with God in the evening."

The setting sun painted the sky in brilliant oranges and purples, reminding him of those precious moments in Elysium. The quiet conversations, the gentle presence of his Creator, the perfect communion that existed before all this strife.

Zophiel's form shimmered beside him, the angel's light softening in sympathy. "Soon, brother, soon."

The angel's words hung in the salty air between them, a promise and a comfort wrapped in three simple words. Enoch closed his eyes, letting the sea breeze wash over him, carrying him back to simpler times.

* * *

Elijah jolted awake on the threadbare mattress, his eyes adjusting to the harsh glare of neon signs filtering through broken venetian blinds. The cacophony of New York City assaulted his senses - car horns blaring, sirens wailing, the constant hum of millions of souls packed into steel and concrete canyons.

He crossed to the grimy window of his Lower East Side apartment, his rough sackcloth garments scratching against his skin. The city sprawled before him, a maze of gleaming skyscrapers and dark alleys. Digital billboards flashed advertisements for the Green World Church's latest initiatives. Hover vehicles zipped between buildings on designated skylines.

"For the time has arrived that the groom claims his bride," Elijah muttered, pressing his weathered hand against the glass. The words felt ancient on his tongue, yet more relevant than ever.

His gaze swept across the urban landscape. Glass and steel towers reached toward heaven like modern-day Babel, their spires disappearing into low clouds. Street level markets bustled with activity as vendors hawked their wares to passing crowds, all bearing the telltale green Mark on their foreheads or right hands.

"Much has changed." Elijah shook his head slowly. "But the word of God will never change."

A brilliant light filled the small apartment, causing the prophet to shield his eyes. When the radiance dimmed, Zophiel stood in the center of the room, wings folded against the low ceiling. The angel's presence made the shabby surroundings feel even more stark and desolate.

The light faded, casting long shadows across the worn floorboards. Elijah's weathered face broke into a knowing smile, the deep lines around his eyes crinkling.

"Zophiel, you shouldn't startle an old man like that." Elijah's voice carried the weight of centuries, yet held a hint of playful rebuke.

The angel's form shifted, seeming to both fill the room and exist beyond its confines. "The time has come, Lampstand. You know the mission - gather whom you can, proclaim the prophecy, until the appearance of the deceiver." Zophiel's voice echoed with the cadence of humanity, yet carried otherworldly authority.

Light coalesced in the angel's hands, materializing into a deep burgundy cloak and a gnarled staff of ancient wood. "Here is a cloak and a staff, and the blessing of the Lord will be upon you."

Elijah reached out, his fingers brushing against the fabric. The cloak felt warm, alive with divine energy. The staff hummed with power as he gripped it, memories of past miracles flooding his mind - the drought, the ravens, the widow's son, Mount Carmel.

The prophet's eyes met Zophiel's, a silent understanding passing between them. The weight of what was to come settled over the small apartment like a heavy mantle.

"What of my brother, Enoch?" Elijah's fingers traced the intricate patterns woven into his new cloak. "Has he found his path in this strange new world?"

Zophiel's form rippled, casting prismatic light across the apartment walls. "The western lands have felt his presence. Through him, the Lord's message spreads like wildfire through the desert. Thousands have cast aside their green Marks, choosing instead the seal of the living God."

"The Green World Church grows desperate, then?" Elijah gripped the staff tighter, feeling its ancient power pulse through his weathered hands.

"They hunt him still, yet cannot touch him. Their prisons cannot hold him, their weapons cannot harm him." Zophiel's voice carried notes of pride and purpose. "Even now, he rests on Patmos, awaiting your arrival when the time is right."

"Patmos." Elijah nodded, memories of John's revelations echoing through his mind. "The isle of visions."

"Your paths will converge soon, when the final battle approaches. But first, each must complete his appointed task." The angel's form began to fade, voice growing distant. "The people of this great city need their prophet, Elijah. Show them the truth that lies beneath the Church's gleaming facade."

Elijah stepped out into the frenetic streets, the burgundy cloak draped over his shoulders like a shroud of ancient authority. The staff in his hand felt as natural as an extension of his own body, a testament to his divine mission.

People rushed past him, lost in their digital worlds, eyes glued to screens that dictated their every move. None spared him a glance. This ancient figure in the sea of modernity. Yet he walked with purpose, a solitary beacon of unwavering conviction.

Above him, the GWC's insignia glowed from towering billboards, their message clear: unity under one church, one Mark, one world. But Elijah saw through the veneer. He knew the truth that lay beneath - a facade crafted to ensnare souls.

His first destination loomed ahead: St. Patrick's Cathedral, an ancient place of worship now overshadowed by skyscrapers and neon lights. Its spires still reached for heaven, a silent protest against the encroaching darkness.

Inside, the hushed reverence of old sanctuaries clung to the stone walls and stained glass windows. The few who prayed within sought solace from the chaos outside. They did not notice Elijah's entrance; his presence was but a whisper among many.

At the pulpit stood a young priest, his sermon laced with references to the GWC's green laws. Elijah's heart clenched at the words — so far from Scripture's truth. He approached slowly, staff tapping against the marble with each step.

The sound caught the priest mid-sentence, and he turned to regard Elijah with curious eyes. The congregation followed suit, a collective intake of breath filling the cathedral as they beheld the prophet.

"Children of God," Elijah's voice resonated through the sacred space, strong and clear despite its softness. "I come bearing witness to His Word - not as it has been twisted by those who would seek to control it for their own ends."

The priest's eyes widened in recognition or fear; perhaps both. He stepped down from the pulpit as Elijah ascended, each step deliberate.

"I speak of a freedom no mark can give or take away," Elijah continued, standing before them all. "The true salvation offered through faith and obedience to God's commandments and repentance of sin through His Son Yahshua."

A murmur rose among the parishioners; some heads nodded while others shook in disbelief or indignation.

Elijah raised his staff; light shimmered along its length and seemed to fill the cathedral with a warmth long forgotten. "Let those who have ears hear," he declared. "For the time of reckoning approaches."

Made in the USA
Columbia, SC
01 February 2025